Above the Best

Above the Best

For the flight training at
Fort Rucker Alabama

Major Dick Hale

authorHOUSE®

AuthorHouse™
1663 Liberty Drive
Bloomington, IN 47403
www.authorhouse.com
Phone: 1-800-839-8640

Published by AuthorHouse   05/17/2012

ISBN: 978-1-4772-0639-3 (sc)
ISBN: 978-1-4772-0640-9 (e)

FOREWORD

IT WAS 1950, the converted LST was plowing the waters of the Pacific, heading towards Korea, when Robert Baker, an enlisted man aboard the ship, was summoned by a Chief Petty Officer to deliver messages to the Signal Officer in the ships ward room. And, it was a moment of truth for Baker. When ushered into the ships ward room Robert became painfully aware that he had somehow been assigned to the wrong part of the ship.

The officer's, that he was only hazily aware of during his day to day duties, were actually sitting at tables covered with linen table clothes, drinking their coffee from china cups while being served by a Philippine stewards mate.

Baker, on the other hand, was eating off of a tin tray, one deck below and under very different circumstances. Different enough, that he decided to change his circumstances, for the better.

That afternoon, Baker submitted his application for flight training with the U.S. Navy. He had always wanted to fly anyway. Baker had actually logged four or five hours a couple of years earlier during his assignment at the Naval Air Station in Jacksonville Florida. He had only quit then because he could no longer afford it.

The applications were submitted, then the Physical examination was scheduled while the ship was in port at Naha Okinawa, The physical was no great problem, except for the nose. "You'll have to get that nose corrected if you plan on wearing an oxygen mask", the Flight Surgeon explained.

After a lot of pain, blood and about ten days in the hospital wearing a kotex under his nose, he was finished with all the formalities. Now, it was just a question of waiting for the orders to arrive.

The U.S. Navy, like any other military organization moves slowly. In this case, they didn't move fast enough. After months of waiting, with no answer to the application, frustration set in, along with the end of his enlistment in the Navy. Not easily deterred, Baker felt it was the Navy's loss and some other service's gain.

After being discharged from the U.S. Navy and reentry into civilian life, the logical approach was through civilian flight training and then a. second attempt at one of the other services. For several years Baker continued with the flight training through civilian means. During this time of flight training, he was fortunate enough to have an excellent instructor in Bill Winslow.

Another piece of good fortune was having a Mother that was interested in flying. Interested enough to purchase a small Aeronautics Champ for Bob and his three brothers who had also become interested in flying after Bob's first few lessons, After a few years flying the champ and anything else that he could wangle, the opportunity to fulfill the dream presented itself.

The Army National Guard had become the answer. Upon finding out that the Guard had a need for "Liaison Pilots", Baker immediately applied.

It had sounded simple, He soon found out that it was necessary to take a battery of tests and a series of home study courses to become eligible for a board of senior officers to interview him to determine his potential as an officer.

After a year as an enlisted man, the home Study courses, and an appearance before the appointment board, Baker had finally achieved his first goal, He was a second lieutenant, A 'butter bar'.

Fresh with his "Sears Roebuck Commission" Baker was ordered to Field Artillery School in Oklahoma. Competition was keen, Baker had a high school education and this course of study required much higher mathematics.

After completing the Field Artillery Officer's basic course, Baker was ordered to primary flight training at Camp Gary, San Marcos Texas, In spite of his high school education he managed to come out in the top 25% of his class in primary flight.

Bob was again fortunate while at San Marcos, He was assigned to Joe Webber, a civilian contract instructor, Joe began to fine tune Bob in preparation for a military career. Joe would say frequently, "when you go on your missions later, you'll want to know this!" At the time, Bob Baker could never understand what missions he was talking about.

Bob had started with a 'stick' of three other primary students at the primary flight school. Due to the high attrition rate and a fatal accident which took the life of Joe Webber and the remaining primary student, Baker was to be the sole survivor of five.

Undaunted by his lack of education (by now he had managed to complete one semester in college), and his method of commission (always to claim, when asked, that it was a. direct commission) Baker completed all of the training the Army could offer in flight schools.

Actually, Baker competed very well because of three special attributes. A stubborn streak, a strong desire to achieve and a natural understanding of flying. Like a duck to water!

After the training was complete and his return to the National Guard unit. Baker's second chance came with a personal letter from the Pentagon asking if he would be interested in entering active duty in the Army, It didn't take long for Baker to make up his mind, he submitted his letter of acceptance that afternoon.

The entry into active duty was at the U.S. Army Aviation Center at Fort Rucker Alabama, with an assignment as a flight instructor in the 'Tactical Division'.

At this point in Baker's flight training he met Clarence Stockwell. "Stock" was a. civil service flight instructor for the Army. His job was to teach aviators how to be flight instructors. Of all of the training Bob had received up to this point, this was the best. Stockwell had a knack for flying like nothing Bob had ever seen. This was to be the fine tuning of his flying career.

Instructing students in the Tactical Division was similar flying to that of a crop duster, with a few exceptions. Baker would eventually spend two and a half years in the back seat of an 0-1 'bird dog' teaching students how to land and take off from the side of hills, in very small confined areas and even off of dirt roads, Areas that seemed impossible to fly into.

CHAPTER ONE

CAPTAIN BAKER EASED the heavy UH1B gunship down onto the skids at the laager area and once he felt the ground, reduced the collective pitch until it was all the way down., slowly rotating the grip for the throttle control until the engine was in idle.

Baker then waited for the exhaust gas temperature to stabilize before rolling the power off for the complete shutdown, While he waited impatiently for the rotors to come to a stop he listened to the sweet sound of the turbines running down, He then undid his shoulder harness and seat belt so that he could get the heavy armor(chicken plate) off of his legs where it had been cutting off his circulation for the last two hours.

As he got out of the helicopter., he thought to himself, "This has been one hell of a day, who was it that said that these little bastards couldn't hit anything?"

Upon walking around the helicopter he observed two, maybe three holes in the rotor blades. Another two holes were in the left side of the aircraft. The two in the front of the aircraft had entered his co-pilots side, passing through the instrument panel and wiping out the top of his cyclic stick, The round took all of the buttons for the radios and rockets before it ricocheted up into the co-pilots lip.

It was one hell of a cross fire, just north of LZ English. No matter which way they turned, they were into another string of automatic AK47 fire.

They had landed just long enough to let the young warrant officer out at the medical tent and as the wounded man got out, he said, "I'm going to ask the old man to put me with someone else, two purple hearts in ten days is too damned many, you're dangerous!".

The Troop Commander had just walked up to Baker's damaged ship and, as usual, was bitching about having another aircraft down, Baker walked off into the underbrush where he undid his gun belt and jungle fatigue trousers, Then, he pulled down his jockey shorts to cut them away with his survival knife.

Once off., the shorts were thrown into the thick underbrush, This was the second time in about two weeks that Baker had crapped his pants during a mission, He was beginning to wonder if it was from the anti-malaria Dapsone pills that they had to take, or was it from the machine gun fire?

Hell, let's face facts, it could be that he was just too damned old for this bullshit. After all, his fellow pilots were in their early to middle twenties and here he was in his first tour of combat at 37. He muttered to himself, "Oh well, you asked for it you dumb ass, now you've got 59 more days to sweat it out!"

ii

After getting his orders changed from Heidelberg Germany to Viet Nam he had nagged the assignments officer at the Pentagon for a helicopter assignment rather than go over as a fixed wing aviator. Baker knew damned well that the helicopter pilots were the ones that really got into the thick of it. "If you're going to go, you might as well go big. No guts, no glory!"

Baker had been a. flight instructor in fixed wing aircraft at Ft. Rucker Alabama when he had received the change in his orders. He had started the process of getting a slot in the qualification course for helicopters. After managing that and the transition into the larger Bell UH1 'Hueys' at Ft. Benning Georgia, Baker had returned his family to Dayton Ohio to wait him out as he started the long trek to South Viet Nam.

The trip to the battle area started at Travis AFB in San Francisco. The military was pumping loads of people into the battle in 1955. Because of the large numbers, the government had gone to contract air lines. Baker's aircraft, along with about 130 other passengers, was a DCS called Saturn Airways, Mot that they were in any hurry, but this was really ridiculous.

Flying to South Viet Nam took days, There were stops in the Philippines, Guam, Wake Island and any other island with a landing area. The only saving grace on the entire trip was a stewardess by the name of Alice, And, Alice was from Dallas. The stewardess was a petite little brunette with big beautiful brown eyes and a body to match. She kept the entire planeload of passengers in an alert posture during the entire trip.

Saturn Airways arrived at Ton Son Nuht airbase and the passengers received their baptism of fire.

During the final approach for landing, the pilot made a. last minute go around. Captain Baker first thought that it was a simple missed approach for landing, only to find out that on short final the aircraft had received automatic weapons fire from the ground.

The next approach was last. Started from i much higher altitude, it was steep and quick in order to provide less exposure time for the enemy fire, It seemed, to Baker, that they almost landed with the brakes locked, as the airplane landed long, with very little runway left.

After what seemed like a very long wait, the Vietnamese ground crew finally got the steps up to the plane for the departure into 'Never Never Land'.

To the uninitiated, the first glimpse of Viet Nam is breath taking. The initial thing to take your breath away is the heavy hot blast of air that is first encountered after getting off of an air conditioned aircraft. The second breath taker is the smell of human shit burning, All of the latrines in Viet Nam appeared to be half of a 55 gallon drum which, when full, was then burned. It was a smell that was everywhere.

Camp Alpha was the replacement center where everyone ended up for assignments, A couple of days at the replacement center was a lifetime.

Officer assignments are handled on an individual basis. Usually, with the officer's career in mind. In Baker's case, he didn't have any background, let alone, much of a career.

So far, Bob had been to artillery school and flight school with one small assignment in between as a flight instructor. So, it was a sure thing that they weren't going to Put Baker anywhere that required any brilliant military background.

When the assignments officer finally called his name, Bob found out that he was going to be assigned to the First Cavalry Division. The assignment officer's voice had appeared sad when he had announced the assignment to Baker. Later, he was to think that the officer was not sad "for me", but sad for the First Cavalry Division.

The First Cavalry was in the central highlands, well north of Saigon and all the 'strap hangers' that went with that city and any other rear area.

The central highlands were as different from the area around Saigon as night is today. Bob was to discover later that it was possible to fly from the beach at the South China Sea to the mountain terrain of the western border of Viet Nam where wild tigers, elephants, monkeys and big snakes roamed. The flight time across the narrow part of South Viet Nam took less than an hour in a helicopter.

From the standpoint of beauty, the northern areas-met the qualifications. It was lush in most parts, and it was a better climate than down south. In the highlands, it actually got cold enough at night to require a blanket and in some areas, cold enough during the day for a sweater under the jungle fatigues.

The arrival at An Khe, home of the First Cavalry Division, was in mid morning. The C139 touched down at the First Cavalry Divisions "Golf Course" which was the name for their airfield. It must have been a shock to the few that had heard of it and arrived with golf clubs, because it was a rock strewn area with aircraft parked everywhere.

The trip to the Division replacement center was quick, and by late afternoon Baker had received his final assignment within the Division.

This time Bob was face to face with the assignment officer, instead of by telephone as in Saigon. The Lt, Colonel looked at Bob's records, snorted, hummed and fiddled with his pipe as he shook his head and finally announced, "I'm sorry, it's going to be necessary to assign you to the First of the Ninth Cav".

Captain Baker saluted and walked out of the tent where a young warrant officer said, "Where ya. been assigned Captin?". When Bob told him, the Warrant Officer said, "Christ, your gonna get a whole wheelbarrow full of medals, if you live thru it!" This came as a shock to Bob since he really knew very little about the First Cavalry Division. After all, he had just learned to spell Captain, without a K.

Baker's arrival in the 1/3th Cavalry area was just in time for dinner where he was introduced to the Squadron Commander who in turn introduced him to his new Troop Commander, Major Black of B Troop. That was a swift hand off, almost like handling a hot potato. Major Black told him to get situated for the night and that he would talk to him about his assignment in the morning.

After a fine meal of "C" rations and a. few "B's"(powdered eggs and milk), Bob began looking around the area to find out where he was going to be billeted.

Whenever he asked the question, "where's the officer billets?", Bob either got a. strange look or a laugh, Bob eventually found out that Camp Radcliffe was a very temporary thing and that the 1/9th was in the rear area of An Kne for the first time in months.

Baker found out that there were no billets. All of the living quarters had been hand built when the troops arrived in country. Each 'hooch' was privately owned. Fortunately, one of the owners was being returned to CONUS (Continental United States) on emergency leave and wouldn't be coming back.

Bob was able to buy his fourth of the hooch for forty dollars, and no closing costs, It consisted of a concrete floor, metal siding with screens at the top, a door and 'early ammo, box' furniture. All in all, it wasn't a bad place, Unfortunately, he wouldn't be there long.

Captain Baker's first night with the 1/9th Cavalry-was educational, First of all, he noticed all of the warrant officers running around wearing black Stetson hats and spurs. Whenever they talked about the past operation in the Ia Drang valley they became glassy eyed. Some of them actually appeared to froth at the mouth.

Baker found out later that evening that the unit had been in one hell of a fight in the Ia Drang valley, losing a lot of people, but had inflicted even heavier damage to 'Charlie'.

Before the night was over, Baker was briefed by the Operations Officer regarding where they had been—and where we were going in the next few days. The Ops Officer was a young Captain who shook his hand and announced. "Welcome to the First of the Ninth, don't plan on going home!"

Sleeping that first night in his new home wasn't easy. It had been a tough day and although he was tired, he had a hard time sleeping, Just as he started to drift off, he heard a strange voice in the distance, "FUCK YOU", "FUCK YOU", After a while, his hooch mates noticed that he was listening and explained that it was the "Fuck You lizard", "Fuck You lizard?" That's right, it was a lizard that inflated a sac under it's ugly chin and then expelled the air. The mating call was a perfect "Fuck You" in the English language.

At about 2 A.M. the next morning, Bob got the second "Fuck You" message when the perimeter was probed by the enemy and they dropped a few of their mortar rounds in. The probe discontinued quickly.

The artillery referred to such action as H&I (harassment & interdiction) fire Captain Baker was an artilleryman and this he understood. It certainly was harassing at two o'clock in the morning.

The next morning Captain Baker was informed by Major Black that he would be assigned as the White Platoon leader, Or, as they said in B Troop, the scout leader. As it turned out, he was going to be the replacement for the present scout leader and would understudy him for a few weeks before the Captain rotated home to the "land of the big PX"

iii

Captain Jack Hawkins was a gutsy guy who had shown his merit while with the troop, first as the grunt commander (infantry) and then as the scout platoon leader. Baker was to get to fly with him for the next few weeks while Jack showed Bob the ropes in the scout helicopter, the OH13S.

The OH13S was nothing more than the Bell 47 with a supercharged engine and added instruments to cover any necessary instrument approaches. Not that the instruments were needed, there weren't many facilities to make approaches to in the highlands. At least any that could be trusted, The OH13S had been in the military inventory for years and was even featured as a medical evacuation helicopter in the TV series, MASH.

Of the six OH13S helicopters in the scout platoon, all had a variety of defensive weapons available to the pilot. Some of the helicopters had eight rockets with 8 pound warheads while others had two M-50 machine guns mounted on the skids.

The sighting devices for the weapon systems were highly sophisticated, Usually consisting of a grease pencil mark on the inside of the Plexiglas's bubble, The mark provided a hit on the target at 1,000 meters, if you sat in the Seat exactly the same way each time you pulled the trigger, And, if you held your mouth right, In spite of all of the inadequacies of the system, the 1/9th scout platoon managed to distinguish themselves, again and again.

Jack started by showing Baker the easy method of finding the enemy, The 1/9th way. It was really very simple, and didn't take a great deal of military training to manage it, So, Bob was able to understand the method right away.

There was nothing to it, The pilot simply hovered around at tree top level in the area where he thought the enemy might be. When they couldn't resist it anymore, they would shoot at you and give their positions away, When they made that fatal mistake, the gunships ships would roll in and smoke them on the spot.

In addition to the outside armament on the OH135, each crew carried a variety of smoke., white phosphorous and fragmentation grenades, All of which were hung on safety wire stretched around the instrument console of the helicopter. The smoke grenades were handy for marking enemy positions, or extraction points for the lift ships picking up the infantry, The fragmentation grenades were for fun.

A little added firepower, was a bomb made from one of the discarded metal ammunition boxes used for shipping rifle ammunition to the field, By propping up the hinged lid. you could drill a perfect hole with a .38 cal, revolver, The hole was the right diameter for the firing device of a hand grenade. The device would be removed from the body of the grenade and screwed into the lid of the ammunition box.

With captured plastic explosive materials, the grenade body, some nails, screws, ball bearings and anything else they could find, the pilots-had one hell of a bomb, However, when the pin was pulled, and the device dropped from the hovering helicopter, the pilot had to be quick on the controls, Any delay, and he could kiss his butt goodbye.

One of the most difficult missions of the white platoon was to stay over the infantry while they were on the ground, This was done to keep the infantry in sight and in constant radio contact.

It didn't sound that difficult until it was tried while they were under a typical dense jungle canopy common to South Viet Nam.

Some areas of Viet Nam the canopy was so thick, it was possible to be S to ten feet directly over the troops and not see them, The troops would know the helicopter was overhead, but they couldn't see the aircraft, and sometimes the pilot could not see them, It was possible to lose the troops completely when they were only a few feet away.

With the thick canopy, the hills and downdrafts, a pilot quickly became very skilled. In the higher elevations, it became necessary to dive down the hillside at tree top level to regain speed and rotor RPM's. They were already low level, too low to lower the collective pitch in order to regain the lost RPM's, The added airspeed assisted in holding the rotor RPM's in the green arc.

iv

The 'Hawk Flight' was another mission of the white platoon, Hawk flights consisted of two scout helicopters low to the ground looking for Vietnamese that were in an area that made them appear a little suspicious. Suspicious in a way that they were either knowledgeable about enemy troop movements, or, were possibly one of the enemy.

One lift ship with an infantry squad, and one gunship was always available for a hawk flight. When a suspect was located, the lift ship would be sent to the coordinates provided by the scout Pilots and the gunship would tag along to provide any fire support required.

Once the area was marked with smoke, the lift ship put the infantry squad on the ground where they secured the prisoner, The lift ship then extracted the entire group to the rear area for interrogation of the suspect. If the prisoner had a logical reason for being in the area, and could prove his answers, he was returned immediately.

Just prior to Jacks departure for the "land of the big PX, the Troop was working a number of hawk flight missions in and around Bong Song as well as the Kontum Province area north of Pleiku.

V

White 12, flown by Lt, Wembley was working the Bong Son area on a hawk flight when he discovered one lone Vietnamese in an area that was far from any villages or roads, The lieutenant made a radio call to the Troop area requesting the lift and gunship team at his coordinates, The gunship arrived at Lt, Wembley's location ahead of the lift ship, It set up a lazy pattern where the crew could roll in, if fire was needed.

"White 12, this is blue leader, we are about five clicks (kilometers) from your present location and we will want smoke," "Roger blue leader, smoke will be out, once you are in sight." "Blue leader, this is white IE, I have you in sight, the smoke is coming out," With that, Lt. Mobley's observer, 5P4 Easley pulled one of the canisters off of the safety wire on the console, pulled the pin and ring, pitching the canister towards the Vietnamese fifteen meters sway.

The Vietnamese was standing with his hands on his head, intensely watching the hovering helicopter a short distance away. He saw the observer toss the gray object out of the aircraft in his direction, The gray canister hit the ground and slowly rolled up to his feet. At that exact moment, the phosphorous grenade exploded, engulfing the suspect, the hovering helicopter, and crew with hot pieces of burning phosphorous.

It was one of those unexplained situations where fatigue or inattention had caused the observer to select the wrong canister, White phosphorous is a tallow like substance that automatically ignites when it comes into contact with oxygen. White phosphorous continues to burn until it is completely consumed, dug out, or is immersed in water.

At this point, the hawk flight became a medical evacuation flight, The Vietnamese lived, The scout crew received severe burns.

vi

Near Kontum, the scout ships encountered a very suspicious situation, While flying low level, the crew noticed a hooch, tucked back into the trees., near a large open valley, Closer examination revealed a canteen hanging in one of the windows along with other military type items

The lift ships had been summoned for pickup of two suspects near the isolated hooch, The hooch was the only one in miles, not like the ordinary villages of South Viet Nam, This group was very suspicious, a n d possibly the enemy.

The troops from the 1/9th had been inserted into a small LZ(landing zone) close to the hooch, They had used extreme caution moving into the hooch, capturing the two suspects without firing a shot, In the hooch, the troops had located the evidence indicating the two were the enemy, A canteen, and a web belt.

Once returned to the rear laager area, by the lift ship crew and infantry, the prize catch of the day was interrogated by a language interpreter, As everyone stood by waiting, the interpreter suddenly away, the suspects were two members of a LEPER colony! They were in the isolated region for a reason.

Baker and the other participants scratched and worried for weeks!

vii

Captain Boston arrived in country shortly after the Troop had set up camp in Kontum. The Captain was a retread from the Alabama National Guard, He was one of the few that had made themselves available for Vietnam by volunteering to leave the safety of civilian life, secure from the draft, and in a weekend pay status.

When he arrived in Kontum. he brought the usual field gear that was issued along with his own personal weapon, in the form of a sawed off, 20 gauge shotgun of the double barrel variety. He scared the hell out of the observers in the white platoon who knew that we were already getting too close to the enemy. How much closer would you have to get to be able to use that scattergun?

Bill Boston was assigned to Baker's tent and when he unpacked his little shotgun with a large supply of number 8 birdshot, Bob asked him if he "wanted to piss the enemy off." Nightly, for a week, Bill would be asked to go to one of the other hex tents to help out with their mosquito problem, using his shotgun for a. swatter.

Bill had been in country for about five weeks when he was assigned a. hawk flight mission not far from the camp area, While flying around some of the low hill areas near Kontum he received some heavy automatic weapons fire in the form of a 12.7 mm (.38 cal.) machine gun Placed on the side of a hill. Captain Boston and his observer were shot down at the foot of the hill mass and under the watchful eye of the enemy machine gun crew.

In spite of the fact that the gunship was in the area within minutes, covering the hillside with rocket and machine gun fire, the enemy gun crew kept Boston and his observer pinned down. They were directly under the barrel of the enemy machine gun, and, because of the crash, the crew was injured badly. This made it impossible to move let alone run.

Captain Boston had sustained a broken back, the observer had internal injuries. It was going to be necessary to get a lift ship in close enough to get the crew out and yet not be in danger of being destroyed by the fire from the heavy machine gun emplacement.

The lift crew commander with infantry squad found a small stream bed directly behind the downed scout ship, which would place the large helicopter with infantry troops, a little further away from the machine gun and directly behind the scout ship. The stream bed offered defilade and the downed scout ship for added cover.

The stream bed was deep enough to completely hide the fuselage of the big helicopter. The negative side of it was that the bed was not wide enough to include the rotor blade plane, It would be tricky to get the body of the helicopter down into the stream bed without a blade strike on the close adjoining banks.

With some very skillful flying, the crew managed to squeeze the aircraft into the stream bed, with the rotor blades overlapping the bank on both sides. This permitted only about six inches of clearance. The infantry squad was then able to drag the crew of the scout back to the lift ship while gunships kept the enemy gun crew occupied with suppressing fire.

Captain Boston's tour in Viet Nam was over. Due to the severity of his injuries, he was medically evacuated back to the States for hospitalization.

viii

Arriving with Boston on the same aircraft from the United States, Lieutenant Carl Wentsworth had become the big subject of discussion almost as soon as the landing gear came up after the aircraft took off from Travis Air Force Base. Wentsworth made a pest of himself on the plane, trying to get the pants off Of every stewardess on the flight.

Lt. Wentsworth was big for an Army aviator, He had tried to enter the aviation program almost immediately after graduating from ROTC at his hometown college. Because of his size, Wentsworth had been turned down, Army aircraft were small and there was a height and weight limit.

But, Wentsworth had an ace up his sleeve in the form of an Uncle Who was a congressman. The lieutenant's next application was not only approved, another officer was bumped from the school so that there would be room for Wentsworth.

Wentsworth's mouth matched his body. It was also big. He attracted a lot of attention with his bragging and boisterous attitude, Because of his size and verbal outbursts, he was well known in the Troop within hours after his arrival.

New arrivals in B Troop would encounter Lt, Carl Wentsworth immediately and he would manage to get their total attention with exploits about the battles he had been in, They would be awe struck, at times, with the details of the battle and the heroics of Wentsworth.

There was only one problem with the Carl's tales. For the first month of his tour in South Viet Nam, Carl was in the gonorrhea ward of the hospital due to a persistent drip, which fit his personality.

Unknown to the new arrivals, the Lieutenant was a habitual liar. The Maintenance Officer, Captain Billy Garner would say. "You can tell when Carl is lying, if you watch him close!" "How?" "By watching his lips, if they're moving, he's lying!"

ix

Skillful flying became an everyday thing with the Pilots of the 1/9th without them realizing that they were becoming some of the best, But in spite of the skills they possessed, they became fatigued before they were aware that there was a problem.

The First Cavalry Division, along with the Army hierarchy, was cognizant of the problem and attempted to put a limit to the amount of flying time a combat pilot should endure during a given month. It was decided that 30 hours per month was the limit. To exceed that, required a waiver.

It was a good plan, except it was doomed for failure in the beginning. The demands for combat missions far exceeded personnel availability, As a result, everyone had to have waivers.

To complete the waivers for each aviators file, the Squadron Flight Surgeon would appear In the field to personally talk to each individual to detect any severe fatigue which might lead to stress and improper decisions. And, to complete the necessary paperwork that negated the 89 hour doctrine.

It became a common occurrence for the aviators to sit patiently while the doctor would ask, "How are you feeling?", "did you have a good breakfast?, "how well did you sleep last night?", "how many flying hours do you have this month?", "do you feel tired?", "are you constipated?", "do you have a drip?".

To each of these questions, the aviators would offer honest answers, appearing to be helpful while the doctor made notes on each of the aviators he interviewed. To the answer about the drip, each would point to Lt. Wentsworth, and say, "No, I don't, but he does!"

When the final question was asked, "Do you feel that you can fly more hours this month?", the Pilots would respond with a positive answer and the doctor would terminate the interview.

Without exception each pilot would say, "O.K. Doc", get up and flap his arms and make putt putt noises as he walked away, or would use his left hand to make the motions as if applying collective Pitch and with his right hand ease the cyclic forward as he rose from a seated position, miming a normal take off in a helicopter. The interviews for waivers were short lived.

Captain Higgens was a recent replacement to the troop and had come from a plush assignment in the United States after his four years at West Point followed by two more years of training as an aviator and in the advanced branch courses.

As in most cases, in the Troop, Higgens was initially assigned to the white platoon. And, had been flying missions on a daily basis.

Higgens and his chase man, WO1 Jacobson were just returning to the laager area after a particularly grueling day of flying the OH13's.

Two hours in an OH13 with the heat, the sweat and the 25 pounds of armor Plate resting oh your legs was grueling. There were many days for the scout platoon pilots that required S to 10 hours of flying.

This had been one of those long days, Captain Higgens made a radio call to his chase, told him that he was going into the "POL point" (refueling point), then started his descent towards one of the two large rubber bladders that contained the hoses and nozzles used for fueling the helicopters.

After Higgens placed the aircraft on the skids near the nozzle he retarded his throttle to ease the aircraft into idle, His observer alighted to get the nozzle for refueling. While the observer was getting ready to refuel, Higgens pulled the aircraft logbook out of the holder and began making the entries for the last flight.

Jacobson had lined his aircraft up with the other nozzle and was into short final on the left side of his leaders aircraft. At about six inches from the ground, Jacobson's advancing rotor blade on the right side of his aircraft came into contact with the retreating blade on Captain Higgens aircraft.

The force of the two rotor blades meeting while going in the opposite direction was so tremendous, that it completely ripped the transmission from its mounts, and then, tossed it into the front seat with Captain Higgens, Higgens was knocked unconscious and remained in a coma for three weeks.

After regaining consciousness, Higgens was released, With the blessing of the flight surgeon, Higgens rejoined the troop in his old capacity as scout pilot.

On his first mission out, during one of the flights common to the scouts, Higgens caught a 12.7mm machine gun round dead center in his chicken plate, The round continued on through to his heart. Captain Higgens was killed instantly.

On this particular mission Higgens had chosen to fly the only OH13 in the troop that had single controls, The observer with Higgens. watched him die and then waited for the ground below to come up to meet the aircraft.

All observers had been taught the basics of how to get a helicopter on the ground in the event something happened to the pilot. In this case., with the pilot slumped over the only controls available, the observer had no options.

xi

Private Nguyen was tired, but in spite of his fatigue, he slipped away from his unit on the outskirts of Chuo Reo and headed for the small stream that he had crossed earlier with his engineer company, A bath would help, He hadn't had an opportunity to really get clean since he and his comrades had left their home if, North Viet Nam.

He dropped his SKS rifle on the bank and took off his issued web belt, the canteen= the rice bag with his daily ration., and then removed his khaki uniform along with his jungle helmet and Ho Chi Minh sandals. The water was cold at first, but his body slowly began to accept it and he eased into the middle of the stream, Nguyen began lathering his body with the soap that he had managed to keep with him these past two and a half months.

Captain Baker and his observer were working a. low reconnaissance of the small river that worked its way north out of the Chuo Reo area. Because of the recent lack of activity, the scout pilots were doing solo work, without chase ships or gunships overhead. It was a boring afternoon, So far, Baker and his observer hadn't seen much worth reporting and were down to their last hour of available fuel before they had to return to the laager area.

Because his regular ship was down for minor repairs, Captain Baker had taken one of the spares with the twin mounted M-60 machine guns on the skids. The machine guns had been test fired earlier in the day and hadn't missed a. stroke when the small thumb button was depressed on the top of the cyclic control.

Nguyen stopped lathering himself, and listened. He could barely hear a faint "whap whap" every once in a while over the noise of the stream, He knew the sound of helicopters, but he couldn't make up his mind whether this was a helicopter or some other noise coming from the jungle, Even if it was a helicopter., he couldn't figure out which direction it was, or how near. Since his arrival in the south he had seen a few helicopters and had also seen what damage they could do.

And then, he saw the helicopter! It was right on top of the trees on the opposite bank arid only a half a kilometer away, heading right at him! "If I can just get to my rifle on the bank!"

Captain Baker saw the figure in the water at the time he rounded the curve in the stream. He saw the man starting to scramble to the bank. A very slight turn to the right brought the OH13S in between the man, and his rifle and possessions on the bank, presenting the opportunity to see that the possessions were those of an NVA soldier.

A rapid turn to the left and another quick pedal turn to the right kept the rotor RPM's in the green and positioned the helicopter for the gun run, Private Nguyen was about mid way between the middle of the stream and the bank when the machine gun fire caught him full in the chest.

As Baker and his observer returned to the laager area, quick notes were made as to location and time of the encounter and Baker's first confirmed KIA (killed in action) of his combat tour. It was also his last flight in the scout ships, he was to be transferred to the gunships.

CHAPTER TWO

THE TRANSITION INTO gunships began after B Troop left the operational area, near the Kontum province. Except for a few sightings and encounters with the enemy., the four weeks hadn't been too lucrative.

WO3 Bob Thacker had been with B Troop from the beginning. He was tired, fed up, ard he was damned sick of seeing the young officers come and go.

In Thacker's opinion, most of the officers had very little military background when they arrived in Viet Nam only to eventually be put in charge of one of the platoons.

Bob Thacker, on the other hand, had over twelve years in the Army when the opportunity for the Warrant Officer flight training program presented itself. It would give Bob the chance for better status and pay, but yet, it would never put him in a position of command.

The problem was that Bob Thacker was very very good as a helicopter gunship pilot. And, he was quite capable of making good decisions. Because of his abilities, Thacker would always be the one that the 'powers to be" selected to provide 'in country' training before turning new officers loose.

"God Damned, Son of a Bitch!" "Why is it always me that you stick these dumb asses with?" "I'm damned tired of having to train every son of a bitch that walks in here!" "What about Froley or one of the other Warrant Officers, they've been here long enough!" Baker stood nearby listening. Finally, the weapons platoon leader, Captain Marshall, said, "Look Thacker, that's and order!".

ii

Thacker said, "O.K. you take it and let's see how you handle a gunship at night". "We'll make a few approaches to the helicopter approach lights at the Golf Course".

The helicopter approach lights consisted of a red and green split beam arranged in such a. manner that a 20 degree descent could be accomplished to the ground by keeping only the green light visible. Over arcing would be evident by seeing an amber light., while under arcing would show a red light, indicating that you were in danger of getting too low.

Thomas set up the first two approaches turning from a base leg to a final leg into the green beam and through smooth control movements, managed to hold the green during the entire final leg without getting a red or amber indication

By the time each approach was completed, he got a "Hmphhh" from the left seat where the aircraft commander, WO Thacker, sat with arms folded across his chest. "Lets see if you can do it one more time, Lucky!"

The third, and final approach was a carbon copy of the first two. Thacker said, "Lets quit for the night Captain". "We'll go out on some missions tomorrow and get this finished up!" Thacker had finally met his match in the seat of a helicopter, And, this officer was a lot older than the rest of the replacements. Maybe Thacker could tolerate him.

For several days, B Troop flew support missions for other units surrounding the An Khe area while Division decided where the best operational area existed for 1/9th type of reconnaissance. During these few days WO Thacker and Captain Baker flew together. Thacker grumbling, Baker still trying to win Thacker's confidence.

They were returning from one of the support missions to the rear area. Baker was at the controls, and, directly behind the red platoon leaders gunship when the round came through the left side of the aircraft. The round struck the armor Plate and splintered into Bob Thacker's left ankle.

Thacker's first reaction was shock, then anger because Baker had been following directly behind the lead aircraft, instead of to the left or right side of the lead.

Once in the rear area Thacker began to realize that he was going to live, and, get a purple heart for a very small scratch, Bob Thacker began to smile for the first time.

Although Baker lost all of the confidence that he had managed to gain up to that point, he gained knowledge about not flying the exact same route as the lead aircraft. And, he began to think that he was blessed with some special luck, He might even be invulnerable!

iii

According to the rules of engagement, the gunship Pilots were hot supposed to fire on anyone unless they could be positively identified as an enemy soldier.

The rules were so strict at one point that the Pilots felt that the enemy had to be in dress uniform, and firing at the gunship in order to return fire. The rules changed on a daily basis and were so stringent that it was almost an impossible situation. The 'VC didn't have such restrictions.

Thomas, his co-pilot and crew were out on a search and destroy mission. The gunship was in an area where the rules were the most strict.

This particular area required a clearance from the Province Chief, the Area Commander for the South Vietnamese Farces and the Area. Commander for the U.S. Forces before an enemy soldier could be fired upon, unless the enemy soldier fired first.

The NVA soldier was in an open area crawling towards the underbrush with his rifle cradled in his arms. Baker and his co-pilot, WO Barrett, frantically changed frequencies on the radios and called the Province Chief and the other required Area Commanders, patiently waiting each time for a final approval (each area had to make certain that they had no friendly forces where the gunship intended to fire).

With each call, and each approval, the NVA soldier was slowly inching his way to a spider hole and security from the gunship, Baker and his crew patiently hovered over the man, watching him make his destination, and safety, just as the final approval was secured. Baker decided, at that point, that a similar situation would not happen again.

iv

Tuy Hoa was on the coast of South Vietnam. The temporary camp (laager) was set up on the sandy beach. It was probably the most decent area Baker had seen since his arrival in Viet Nam. At least it was wide open. There was no cover for the enemy to move into position for an attack. From the standpoint of mortar positions, they didn't have any. Also, here was a chance to get into the South China Sea for some swimming.

The only problem with Tuy Hoa, was wind. It blew in constantly from the ocean, making it tough to keep the helicopters at a never when they were heavily loaded. If the helicopter was turned with the tail into the wind, the rotor blades would lose lift and the aircraft would settle to the ground.

It was necessary to keep the nose into the wind at all times, always remembering to shut the aircraft down into the wind, to prevent a 'hot start'.

A Hot start was one of the major problems that pilots watched for during the engine starting process. The engine temperature rose rapidly to the 800 centigrade red mark during starting. If it did not return to the green mark quickly, the engine could melt in its housing. With the Wind blowing up the tail pipe, the cool air, headed for cooling the engine, was insufficient volume.

In addition to the hovering and starting problems which caused damage and additional maintenance work for Captain Billy Garner, the blowing sand always presented a problem at the mess hall. The meals during the stay at Tuy Hoa were always gritty.

Malaria was another problem for the First Cavalry Division because of the wet steamy jungle that everyone lived in. At one point, the Troop was 75% infected with malaria or black water fever.

In and attempt to combat the malaria, the military introduced an experimental drug. Everyone was required to take it.

The dapsone pill was taken on a daily basis. A very large Orange pill was also taken once a week. The pills were ingested at the entrance of the mess tent, under the watchful eyes of the medical personnel.

The dapsone pill caused severe cramps along with dysentery. As soon as Bob awoke in the morning, he'd throw back the mosquito net. check his boots and put them on, quickly heading for the nearest latrine where he would find three or four other people waiting in line ahead of him.

Everyone in line was doubled over in excruciating pain. Discussions would then begin about who had the greatest need and who was in the worst pain. On one occasion Bob heard one man offer 200 piasters to allow him to go to the front of the line. Many didn't make it in time to the fifty gallon drum latrine.

In spite of the pills, many members of B Troop came down with malaria and were 'med-evaced' to the States or Japan for treatment. In some cases, the fever was so high that it was necessary to pack the infected trooper In ice.

The Commanding General of the Division finally issued an order. "You will not get malaria". But, he forgot to tell the mosquitoes.

vi

The 1/9th Cavalry had been moved into the Tuy Hoa area, in Phu Yen Province in support of the First Cavalry Division operations Deckhouse, Nathan Hale and Henry Clay.

It was mid June of 1965, Captain Baker had been in country nearly 50 days. During that first two months, he had received a number of hits in the OH13S, been involved in several good battles and had seen one co-pilot wounded. During this time, he had been tagged with the nickname 'Magnet Ass'. He always seemed to draw fire when no one else did.

It was also during this time that Baker became the Platoon leader of the weapons platoon. This put him in control of the six guns-hips, the crews and the assignments for missions.

Because of the hits that Bob was taking in his aircraft, he began to develop a close relationship with the Maintenance Officer. Captain Garner.

Billy would watch for Baker to come back from a mission and would be near the landing pad in order to quickly assess the battle damage and repair it so Bob could get back into the air, Often, quick turn around was needed. In that case, the maintenance personnel used the '80 knot tape', A green tape that covered the holes, but managed to stay on, even at 80 knots.

Bob began to wonder if Billy just Wanted his 'goody packages' arriving from the States, Or he was getting tired of buying Bob cokes. Then again. Bob wondered if Billy was conducting a. study to see how often a pilot could get his aircraft shot up without running out of skill and ideas all at the same time.

vii

A common practice among pilots was to make deals on personal possessions such as Coleman lanterns, a captured pistol or machine gun or maybe a stereo system not yet shipped back to the States.

The evening before a hairy mission, Baker might approach another pilot, saying, "In case you don't get back tomorrow, can I have your Coleman lantern?". Billy Garner always asked if he could have Captain Bakers pistol in the event he caught 'the right round'.

It was almost a year since the Division had arrived in country. Most of the Officer and enlisted replacements arriving, were slated for the First Cavalry Division.

Captain Pete Prosen arrived in country and along with many other replacements, was sent to the First Cavalry Division.

In many cases, this was not a welcome assignment. By now the TV and newspaper coverage of the war in South Viet Nam was headline material, And. the First Cavalry Division was getting a lot of media, attention in the headlines, B Troop specifically was getting more than their share of the coverage. By now, the Troop was being referred to at home as "Barnes Bravos".

Pete Prosen was one of those that was unusually nervous about the assignment to B Troop. As it turned out, more nervous than most, It took one casual statement to make up Pete's mind.

The Troop was between missions. It was one of those days when they had fresh food. The real stuff instead of the C's or a. combination of the C rations and powdered meals. Everyone was In a crazy mood because of the fresh food and a chance to 'stand down' for the day. Billy Qamer was slightly insane anyway, maybe more so than the rest of the pilots.

Billy was standing in the chow line with Baker when Pete Prosen exited the Troop Commanders tent and started for the mess tent.

Someone shouted., "Hey look, there is the new replacement that just arrived!" As Pete got closer, he could see the glassy eyes staring at him from just above the dark circles.

At that time Billy broke the silence, the chow line, and wind, Billy fan towards Pete waving his arms like a mad man, yelling, "Everyone stand back, I just want to shake this man's hand before he goes out and loses it!".

At this point, Pete Prosen did a complete about face, without losing stride, marched back to the Commanding Officer's tent where he promptly tore his wings off of his fatigues. Major. "I refuse to fly!".

Maybe that was one way to get rid of the cab drivers. Unfortunately, Prosen was a regular Army officer who had intended to make the Army his career.

viii

During the stay in Tuy Hoa, Billy Garner and Bob began exchanging goody package contents received from the States. They were always a welcome thing to get, because the food wasn't that appetizing at times.

By the time the packages arrived in South Viet Mam, what was cookies or cake when mailed from home, would arrive as a box full of crumbs and ants. And sometimes, even the ants were good.

Often, it was necessary to eat lunch while on a mission. There were days when the missions were back to back, requiring that you carry a. box of C rations with you to eat while flying. If you were lucky enough to be able to land somewhere for a few minutes, the meal could be heated, making it a little more palatable.

The C rations came in different varieties. From beans and franks to turkey loaf, Besides the main meal, the box contained a small can of peanut butter, some jam, a can of fruit cake or bread, a can of fruit cocktail (if your were lucky), a pack of four cigarettes, a napkin and some toilet paper. The C rations also contained instant coffee mix with powdered cream and sugar, or a package of chocolate mix.

The bread was never very satisfying to Baker, but it provided the opportunity to make a stove to heat the rest of the rations. By punching small holes around the bottom rim of the can and removing the lid, the contents could be soaked with JP-4 (jet fuel) from the main drain of the helicopter, Once lit, it provided a perfect stove for heating the rest of the meal.

Baker also discovered that he could place a can in the exhaust section of the jet engine and heat his lunch, A sudden mission would result in a small explosion when the can exploded from the heat.

The most refreshing drink was the chocolate mix. That, along with two of the coffee creamers and a package of sugar for added sweetness. The hot chocolate and the peanut butter is what kept Bob alive. In spite of everything, he went from 159 pounds to 129 pounds in the first three months of his tour.

ix

The missions for the operations in Tuy Hoa were scattered over a large area. The Troop was put in support of many units of the First Cavalry Division.

By this time, the pilots in the 1/9th had become known by tN4r-will—signs, and because of their abilities with the weapons, would receive requests from the units on a personal basis through radio messages.

Baker had been flying the gunship with the 2 rocket pods, each carrying nine of the 2.75" folding fin aerial rockets. The 40 mm turret just beneath the nose had become his cup of tea. As weapons platoon leader, he felt that each pilot should have his own choice of weapons and become skilled with it.

The turret for the short 40 mm cannon was operated from the left seat of the aircraft with a twin pistol grip recticle sight. The turret moved, within certain limits, by moving the twin pistol grips. Where the turret sight was pointed, the cannon pooped the exploding grenades out, on target, at a rate of 250 rounds per minute.

The grenades were 'spin armed'. When the launcher fired them out of the short barrel, the lands and grooves of the barrel started a stabilizing spin of the grenade, which in turn armed the projectile.

When the grenade struck the ground, or twigs, the point detonating fuse exploded it into a fifteen meter radius. The small pieces of shrapnel looked a lot like the flint wheel from a Zippo lighter.

The belted grenades were in a box behind the two front seats. They passed through a chute between the seats to the "chunker" under the nose of the helicopter.

The box had a normal capacity of 250 rounds of the belted 40 mm ammunition. Baker had modified the capacity to 400 rounds to permit a little more time over the target area.

The added rounds presented a problem. Because of the additional weight forward of the center of gravity, the aircraft was nose heavy. Approaches required a light touch. Any roughness on the controls could be disastrous. The cyclic stick had to be back against the stop to keep the aircraft level. A normal approach was with cyclic stick all the way to the rear, using collective as a primary means of making the approach.

X

Baker's reputation as a gunship pilot caught up with him. He had received a call from one of the aviation units assigned to another unit in the Division. "Red charger 22, this is Gunner 11". "Roger, gunner 11, this is red charger 22". "Red charger, I'm in an unarmed helicopter north of you and receiving sniper fire from a tree near the Song Bhe river, can you give me a little help?". Roger gunner 11, we're on the way!".

Baker's co-pilot located the observation aircraft just as they approached the river and pointed it out to Bob. Bob gave the observation helicopter a call, telling him to mark the tree with smoke and then he called his chase ship, red 23 and told him to follow the lead ship in.

When the red smoke appeared, it was just beneath a very large tree along the bank of the river. The tree was so dense the crew couldn't see the sniper. Captain Baker called his chase pilot and told him that they would start at the top of the tree with the 40 mm rounds and work their way down to the base of the tree. The firing would be accomplished in a very wide eight pattern.

Baker started his run first, firing 15 to 20 rounds of the exploding 40 mm shells at the top of the tree and then, slowly turned to the left, followed by a wide right turn back to make a run at the opposite side of the tree while red 23 was making the original run established by Baker.

By doing it this way, the gunships were coming in opposite directions, within seconds of each other, firing from both directions at the same time.

After about 20 minutes of firing in this pattern, with short 15 to 20 round bursts, the tree was stripped bare of all foliage and the sniper. The observation helicopter landed and picked up the sniper's rifle that was at the foot of the tree.

xi

Captain Billy Garner's eyes would light up and he would cock his partially bald head. With his southern drawl, he would say, "You can almost hear those NVA soldiers running down the Ho Chi Minh trail, their racing slicks just a zingin!".

Billy was right, they were pouring into South Viet Nam at a tremendous rate, on trucks, bicycles, and on foot. The racing slicks that Billy was referring to were the Ho Chi Minh sandals. The bottom part of them were made out of old tires, with tread still on them. The straps were made out of the inner tubes.

Russian made trucks were caught in the open once in a while, but early in 1966 and 1967, most of the activity was with foot soldiers. Occasionally a crew would catch an NVA soldier, in the open, and on a bicycle. The latter was the situation with LT. Wentsworth and his co-pilot during the operation to the north of Tuy Hoa.

Lieutenant Wentsworth had caught a glimpse of the NVA soldier riding the bicycle, through a break in the trees. Four pair of rockets were fired immediately since the soldier was in a designated 'Free Fire Area', only to strike the tree tops and burst too high to do any damage to the cyclist.

Wentsworth and his co pilot continued to search the area for the man, glimpsing him now and then, but not getting a clear shot. "Keep your eyes open back there!" Wentsworth advised his door gunner and crew chief. "That goddamned slope is still in that woods somewhere, and if we can hang in long enough, he'll come out!".

The cyclist, instead of stopping in the security of the dense area, continued his travel into the opening.

Wentsworth and his co pilot circled back to the left for a complete 360 degree turn to suddenly see the NVA soldier in the open area.

"Son of a bitch, would you look at that, he came out of the woods!" Wentsworth then told his door gunners to offer covering fire on both sides of the helicopter as he started the dive for the next rocket run.

Just before he squeezed the trigger for another pair of rockets, Wentsworth changed his mind. The helicopter continued the descent to about four feet off of the ground and at the last minute, Wentsworth put it into a 'slip' (the aircraft travels sideways, and forward at the same time).

The NVA soldier had just about made it to the next group of trees, and cover, when the metal landing skid on the helicopter, hit him in the back of the head, at 30 knots airspeed.

xii

Baker and his co-pilot WO1 Barrett were in one of the valleys west of Tuy Hoa and in support of an infantry unit from the First Cavalry Division.

Not much had happened throughout the morning. The infantry unit was on a 'search and destroy' mission, and although there was occasional radio chatter with the gunship over them, there was never any request for close support fire from the helicopter.

"Red charger 22, this is classy six. Can you land to pick up captured documents?" "Bullshit", Baker thought, that's not our mission. Then again, he had been working with this particular ground commander off and on for a week. He had been easy to support. Not like some of the ground troops who never seemed to understand that you had to return to your rear area, once in a while, to get fuel.

"Roger Classy Six. pop smoke for the pickup point, and we'll extract the documents". The white smoke wafted from the edge of the wooded area where the U.S. Troops were located. The approach to the small clearing, was set up, and executed quickly.

The gunship touched down just as the GI came running out from the woods and stuffed a canvas knapsack through the left window. The GI grinned, waived and then returned to the woods. Classy six called again and said that he didn't think he would need the gunship anymore and they could return to the laager area.

After reaching altitude, Baker finally opened the knapsack. It was stuffed full of South Vietnamese currency, in varying packets. The smaller packets contained 300 piasters, and were on top of the knapsack. About two thirds of the way down, the packets got thicker, until the held 500 to 700 piasters. Bob determined that the infantry had captured the payroll for an enemy unit.

Baker counted the piasters and found that they had over a thousand U.S. dollars in value.

By the time Baker and his crew got to the rear area, the knapsack contained 600 dollars worth of Piasters. Each of the four crew members got 100 U.S. Dollars worth for spending money.

In the rear area, the money was turned into U.S. intelligence, and the receipt for the money was then turned over to the Troop Commander.

Some months later, the Troop Commander received a thank you letter from the South Vietnamese in Saigon. "Thanks for the 100 dollars in piasters". Apparently, each person that handled the money, had removed his cut.

xiii

It was near Highway 1 where the two NVA were first spotted, running in and out of the trees, heading northwest. For about fifteen minutes they would be visible for a split second and then disappear in the breadfruit and coconut trees. Baker and his crew had about given up on seeing them again when all of a sudden they burst into the open, running across a. rice paddy.

The two enemy soldiers, were in a free fire area, and they were both carrying weapons while they ran, at full speed, for the far corner of the rice paddy.

Baker quickly unhooked the 40 mm gun sight from its locked position on the ceiling of the helicopter and moved it into position, His copilot WO1 Barrett completed the turn to start the gun run.

By this time, the two enemy soldiers were about midway in the rice paddy, "Chunk, chunk, chunk", the grenade launcher wasn't missing a beat, but, the 40 mm rounds were exploding at the heels of the two NVA as they ran at top speed across the paddy.

Baker was having a hard time getting the rounds in any closer, it seemed the rounds were twenty meters behind the pair each time they exploded.

He could see the dirty little puffs of black smoke, the flash, the muddy water, but never close enough for an effective hit. There wasn't much time, they were about the reach the tree line and safety. Baker just couldn't seem to catch up with them.

Just as the two soldiers reached the corner of the rice paddy, and within a few feet of the next entanglement of trees, they stopped. Both turned around and knelt down., raising the French made 9mm machine guns to return fire on the gunship. At that precise moment, the 48mm fire caught up with them.

xiv

Damage assessment missions were assigned to the pilots of the 1st of the 9th Cav on an infrequent basis. Captain Baker managed to be on two of these missions during the time the troop was working the areas around Tuy Hoa.

Bob was flying chase aircraft for the Troop Commander on a. damage assessment mission for an 'Arc Light Raid'. Major Barnes was in the C k C (Command and Control) helicopter. They were to move into a large suspected enemy stronghold immediately after the B-52's had emptied their payload of 500 pound bombs into the area.

For some reason, Major Barnes radioed Baker's ship, "Red 22, this is Red Charger Six, stay off to the east, to cover me, I'll go in low level and do the assessment!". "Roger, red charger, will do!". Baker and his crew listened to the radio frequency assigned by the Air Force and when the message came that the bomb bays were empty, they watched as Major Barnes flew into the area that had just erupted with smoke, fire and uprooted trees.

The helicopter had barely reached the center of the impact area for the bombs, when all hell broke loose and the ground all around the command and control ship began to erupt all over again. A second load of bombs had been dropped from the B-52's who were barely visible as slight contrails in the sky overhead.

Through a lot of luck and some fast maneuvering, Major Barnes managed to get his helicopter out of the total devastation without damage to the crew or helicopter.

Baker's second damage assessment flight was in an area near the original Arc Light Raid. Only this time, it was an assessment for an artillery raid.

Baker and his crew laid off from the area while the field artillery conducted a 'time on target' artillery raid into a suspected enemy area. Artillery pieces from several battalions were involved using high angle or low angle fire as necessary.

Depending on their distance from the target area, each artillery unit was to place rounds into the suspect area, all at the same time.

This was accomplished by mathematically figuring the time of flight of the rounds. With that information, and the location of the target, the data is fed to the artillery pieces. With reduced or increased charges for the rounds, and artillery Piece elevations, all rounds are supposed to arrive on target.

"Red 22, this is Illuminator 3, rounds complete, and tubes clear!". "Roger Illuminator 3, understand tubes are clear?" "Roger red 22, I repeat, the tubes are clear!!".

Baker started their descent to tree top level from the stand off position and began entering the target area to assess the damage.

Just as the helicopter reached the center of the impact zone, the ground began erupting again, all around the gunship and at the same time, "Red 22, Red 22, this is Illuminator 3, we have a battery that fired a late volley!!"

As Baker's helicopter cleared the area, he called the artillery unit. "Illuminator 3, this is Red 22, we are clear of the area, and returning to our unit, no damage assessed". Baker continued, "If this ever happens to me again, I will personally land in your area and look you up. And I do carry a. gun!" That was the last time Baker was ever requested for damage assessment.

CHAPTER THREE

THE WORD ALWAYS came unexpectedly. Platoon leaders were called to the operations tent for a briefing and told to be prepared to move out the following morning.

Moves by air, in helicopters, were not the easiest accomplishment under the circumstances. There was always an advance party with a "Jump CP" (command post), followed by the main body carrying all of their possessions, that could be carried safely, in their aircraft.

The scout platoon, in their small helicopters, had it worse than anyone during a move. Their gear had to be thrown on another aircraft in the Troop. It might be days before they found everything that was theirs, after arriving at a new camp.

When they did arrive in a new area, the operations tent, mess tent and living tents would go up first. Then, as time permitted, the members of the Troop would go through the motions attempting to make the place look like home.

Wooden boxes that the rockets arrived in became premium items during the first week at a new laager area. They were used to make a flat pallet for the air mattress, with the remaining scraps of wood used as supports for the much needed mosquito netting.

Additional ammunition boxes would be used for storage areas near the sleeping pallet and became referred to as "early ammo box furniture". Sand bags would be filled, drainage areas around the tent dug, latrines and piss tubes installed.

When a new campsite (laager) was established, it was easy to tell who was close to the time that they would be rotated home, the area surrounding their tent would have more sandbags than anyone else.

Because of the weight limit, almost everything that was not a. personal possession had to be destroyed before a move could be completed. Once camp was broken, there was nothing left behind that the VC or the NVA could use. With the exception of the 'piss tube'.

A camp recently abandoned would look strange with the piss tubes still in place. The heavy cardboard container for the rocket motors, was used extensively for this purpose, Placed in the ground at about 30 degrees, they were perfect for the pause that resfreshes. They were always at a number of convenient locations throughout the Troop area.

ii

This was going to be a big move. Bravo Troop was moving back into the Pleiku area for Operation Paul Revere and in support of the 2d and 3d Brigades of the Division. It would be the first time that the Troop had returned to the Ia Drang valley since Baker had arrived in country.

The laager area was near "the plantation" on the outside of the Army stronghold at Pleiku. The plantation was a large area of rubber trees owned by Michel in. B Troop personnel were given strict guidance not to damage any of the trees or the Army Would have to pay for them.

Operations in and around Pleiku continued for a month or so in support of the Brigades, with a number of temporary moves, for B Troop. Short moves to other, more temporary, locations so the Troop could be closer to the area they were operating in.

The area directly around Pleiku was a large plain. The plain was just to the west of the First Cavalry Division home base of An Khe, and adjoined the road where the French had taken a severe beating in the fifties, remembered in the history books as 'Dien Bien Phu'. The road that ran between An Khe and Pleiku still had the tank hulls and destroyed half tracks alongside.

The only striking thing about the Pleiku plain was 'titty mountain', or 'pussy mountain', depending on which direction you looked at it. It consisted of two relatively large twin hills next to each other which would give the appearance of a nice pair of 36 breasts from one side.

From the other side, with the tree growth, surrounding the gentle slope and the slit that split the two hills, it was called "pussy mountain".

iii

Flying support for the 2d Brigade had not been too fruitful for Baker until one day while in the area assigned, he received a radio call, "Red charger 22, this is Blaster 6, over." Blaster 6, this is Red Charger 22, go ahead, over." "Roger Red Charger, we have just seen a large squad of VC run into the elephant grass at coordinates 230650, and we are receiving fire from that area!".

Baker's co-pilot, WO1 Barrett, checked the map they always carried on the missions and headed in the direction of the coordinates.

Upon arriving, the gun crew found that they were in a large open area. The exact location of the enemy was a. three acre square marshy area with 4 foot elephant grass.

Baker made another call to Blaster 6. "Blaster 6, this is Red Charger 22, we are in the area, would you mark the target with smoke so that we have a positive fix?" "Roger Red Charger 22, we'll mark it with white smoke!" The command and control helicopter made a quick low pass and the white smoke appeared dead center in the marshy area.

Captain Baker made a call to his chase ship, Red Charger 12. "Red Charger 12, this is Red Charger 22, we're going to take care of this area like we're planting potatoes. Follow my lead!"

Baker had his co-pilot start a shallow dive towards the the marshy area while he got the 40 mm firing device ready, The co-pilot was told to start along one side, break to the left and then return on the other side of the square going in the opposite direction.

They were at about four feet above the marshy area as they started the run from north to south. As they approached the northern edge, Baker squeezed the trigger and the 40mm gun started it's 'chunk, chunk, chunk'. At 250 rounds per minute, it would take about a minute and a half to unload the 400 round capacity. The chase ship would have another minute available with no misfires.

The exploding shells were hitting the ground from both sides of the fourteen people that had entered the marshy area and spraying shrapnel in a fifteen meter radius with each explosion. In about a 60 second flight, it was all over for the large squad of armed VC that had taken sanctuary in the tall grass.

When Baker landed at the refueling and rearming area after the flight, the Command and Control ship landed behind them. Blaster 5 came over to thank the B Troop crew and then asked Baker if he could count one of the kills for his own aircraft. Baker wanted to tell him that it was hard to accomplish a kill from 3.000 feet away, but didn't.

iv

It was the beginning of the monsoon season and it rained constantly. The 'hex tents' were never designed for much, let alone rain. They had absolutely no water repellent capability.

Baker, along with Lt. Wentsworth and WO1 Barrett shared the same small tent. It leaked constantly. Getting to sleep was tough enough for Baker as it was, without the constant dripping of water somewhere in his bed.

Baker had written to his wife asking that a plastic drop cloth be mailed to him so that he could stretch it over his mosquito netting at night. He had also mentioned that he had a severe case of dysentery from the dapsone pills and requested something to solve the problem.

Baker had just returned from a mission and found the package on his bunk along with several letters from home. He opened the package to find his drop cloth that he needed, plus one package of assorted sizes of corks!

That night it rained harder than usual. The drop cloth, just over the mosquito netting, started collecting the water drops throughout the night, until nearly a gallon of water had accumulated. The entire gallon let loose at 3 a.m. full in the face of Baker who was dreaming of Alice from Dallas.

V

Baker and his crew, along with Lt. Wenstworth as chase had been working out of the special forces camp west of the Michelin plantation for several days. The special forces camp was just across the river from the Laotian border. All of the missions had been in support of the special forces personnel during their long range patrols.

The gun team had just returned to their home laager area for the night when a call was received from the special forces camp that they had a "LRP team" (long range patrol) surrounded and receiving fire. They needed to be extracted immediately.

Major Barnes in his command and control aircraft, one lift ship with infantry, Captain Baker and his chase Lt. Wentsworth cleared the laager area just as the sun was setting.

It was normally about a 20 minute flight to the special forces camp. But the group was about to encounter real problems. As the sun wasted away for the day, the fog began to build. It was to become a very heavy fog before the night was over.

Night flying in Viet Nam is like no other place in this world. Normally, during the night, a pilot can detect some light from cities or towns and as a result, have some indication of where he is in relation to where he wants to go. Rural electrification never made it Viet Nam. It was the darkest place in the world. The fog compounded it.

Major Barnes and the lift ship became separated from the two gunships almost immediately. Having been there several times in the past few days, Baker at least, had some general idea of where the camp was located. He headed that direction.

Major Barnes and his lift ship were in direct contact with the two gunships during the flight when it became evident that something was wrong. Major Barnes was fading out slowly as each communication was made between the helicopters.

Captain Baker radioed, "Red Charger 5, this is red charger 22, we are approaching the landing area".

"What is your location?" "Roger red charger 22, we are not that certain of the camp location, and we don't have you in sight!" Baker had detected that Red charger six's signal was getting weak and called again. "Red Charger 6f your signal is very weak, what heading are you on presently?"

There was a long pause, and then a very weak response. "Red charger 22, we are on a. heading of 230 degrees". Baker knew that he was somewhere in the vicinity of the special forces camp and that the major was west of him. In Laos.

"Red charger six, this is red charger 22. Suggest you check your directional gyros and your magnetic compass, I believe you may be out of country!"

There was another long pause and then a very weak response, "Red charger 22, roger your message, we seem to have a little difficulty here!" "We are doing a one eighty (turning around) and will have to head for fuel!"

By this time, Captain Baker and his chase, Lt. Wentsworth, were over the special forces camp. The fog was extremely heavy in most areas, with an occasional break. Radio contact with the special forces personnel confirmed that they were in the right area because the 'green berets' could hear the helicopters.

The UH1 helicopters had a powerful searchlight capable of movement up, down, left and right from the pilots collective pitch control. The thumb button, on WO1 Barretts side of the aircraft was moved back and forth in an attempt to locate a familiar land mark.

Baker radioed his chase, "Red 12, this is Red 22, we found the camp!" "It is right under us in the break in the fog, follow us in!" Captain Baker put the helicopter in a steep descent, while WO Barrett continued the use of the landing light in the small break of the fog bank and both helicopters, tight together, completed their approach into the special forces camp.

Once safely on the ground, Captain Baker contacted the Green Beret commander to find out the situation. "The last we heard from our LRP patrol, they were on top of this hill, and under fire". The special forces Captain was pointing to a small hill top on the map and continued to explain the situation, "Our man has 14 Ruffpuffs (RFPF, Regional Forces, Popular Forces)with him and believes that the enemy force will attack tonight, under cover of darkness!"

Captain Baker explained that there was no possible way to get out of the special forces camp and find the hill with the fog, The special forces captain confirmed that the man with the RFPF's had just reported in his last radio message that the hill was enveloped in fog.

The decision was made to maintain radio contact throughout the night., and at the moment the fog lifted, extract all of the personnel from the hill top with the gunships.

The UH1B gunship was designed for four personnel only, with a slightly beefed up engine to carry the extra, weight of the armament systems, By removing all of the rocket pods, the 40mm belted ammunition and box from both ships it was barely possible to pick up an additional seven men in each gunship, provided they were small and light in weight.

Both crew chiefs and gunners worked frantically to remove the armament systems in preparation for the extraction from the hilltop while Baker and Wentsworth talked to the special forces commander and operations officer.

The special forces LRP advisor was contacted on the radio and told to start cutting trees down on top of the hill in preparation for an LZ (landing zone) and told as soon as the fog lifted, they would be extracted.

Lt, Wentsworth bedded down with one of the Montgnard females (Mont-yard, the lower level of the caste system of Viet Nam, who stayed at the camp. She had betel nut (a narcotic) blackened teeth, shining like a black moon. The remainder of the crews stayed with the helicopters, sleeping on the ground and in a sitting position in the aircraft. And, they waited.

The break in the fog came shortly after sunrise. The two helicopters took off for the location of the RFPF team, locating the hill immediately. The landing zones that were cut the night before were half the size they needed to be. "Squirrel 14, this is Red Charger 22". The special forces team leader replied, "Go ahead red charger 22, we're sure glad your here!"

"Squirrel 14, I have a little bad news for you. the LZ's are way too small to get into". "You have no choice, you will have to come down off of the hill and into the valley below for extraction". (Silence) "Squirrel 14, we will stay over you at tree top level on the way down the hill, but you will have to hurry, we will be low on fuel!"

The special forces advisor and his RFPF's started the trek down the hill as Baker and his chase gave them cover with their door guns.

By the time the 14 personnel were in an area for extraction the two helicopters had burned off additional weight in fuel consumed. Seven men were loaded on each of the two UH1B's and each of the helicopters lumbered out of the slightly wooded valley back to the special forces camp.

Captain Billy Garner was waiting for the return of Red 22. When Bob Baker landed, Billy was surprised to find no battle damage. "Hell, he'd screw a bamboo viper, if someone would hold it for him!" Billy responded when Baker told him of Wentsworth climbing in bed with the Montgnard woman. "If she hadn't been all strung out on that damned betel nut, she'd probably turned him down!"

Major Barnes debriefed Captain Baker as soon as the crew had a meal for the first time in a day and a half. "Did you receive any fire while you were extracting the special forces group?" When told no, Major Barnes had said, "That's too bad in a way, I was going to put you in for a Distinguished Flying Cross!"

"You would think that we would have gotten some thanks for the mission" "The special forces camp commander or the team leader of the RFPF's hardly bothered to say goodbye, let alone thanks!" Billy Garner readily agreed with Captain Baker. "Other units in country are passing out medals for far less, and we have a Troop Commander that considers a mission like that to be an everyday occurrence." "Not a damned one of us is going to get anything out of the chances we took!" Baker proved to be wrong, Lt. Wentsworth developed another persistent drip.

vi

As usual, it was pitch black and it was raining when Captain Baker got the word that there was a briefing in the operations tent, He was writing a letter home to thank his wife for the corks, He blew out the candle and got his boots on for the trip to the operations tent

Because of the blackout conditions of the camp area Baker didn't see the foxhole. All of a sudden the earth left the bottom of his jungle boots and he was shoulder high in the ground with two broken ribs and some heavy scratches on his side that would develop into ringworm.

vii

"Main rotor clear, clear right and clear left", the door gunner and crew chief repeated, "clear right, clear left". Baker continued with the check list as WO1 Barrett went through the procedures. "voltmeter 2E volts, starter engage and check clock". Baker still thrilled at the sound of the big Lycoming 1100 horsepower engine as it began winding up, the igniters clicking and the sudden whoosh as the raw JP4 ignited.

It had been a rough night as they broke camp in preparation for their move to a special forces camp outside of the Ia Drang valley. A place called Plei Me was the subject of the briefing the night before. Baker had gone to the medical tent right after the briefing to get his ribs taped and had begun getting the platoon gear together for the move.

The briefing had been short, but to the point. The new Troop executive officer, Major Saunders had briefed the platoon leaders, and other personnel on the developments. From intelligence had come the word that a large contingent of NVA had been making their way down the Ho Chi Minh trail into the south via the Ia Drang. Yet. the special forces contingent at Plei Me had said.

"There isn't any enemy activity within miles of here, we've cleaned them all out!".

Major Saunders had arrived in the Troop just a few days earlier. He was personable and seemed to be understanding about the problems of the men of the Troop. Where Major Barnes was hard and seemed to be unfeeling about the needs of the men, Saunders had been the opposite. It was going to be a welcome relief when Saunders became the Troop Commander. His understanding ways along with his nice smile and white teeth seemed to relax the people around him. His background would also benefit the Troop. He was a graduate of West Point.

The trip to Plei Me was only a. twenty minute flight from the Pleiku area and the arrival was quick and orderly. The operations section of the Troop was set up in the special forces camp where the personnel of the section also bedded down. As usual, the camp commander and the resident green berets were living high on the hog. The camp was electrified by a generator which provided the residents with refrigerators, air conditioning and all the pleasures of stateside living.

The perimeter defense for the special forces camp was typical. They had the large rolls of concertina wire, the foo gas, claymore mines, and the punji stakes dipped in water buffalo shit. B troop would be outside of the buffalo shit, with their own defense.

Foo gas consisted of a concoction much like napalm. It was in a fifty-five gallon drum. The drums were placed in strategic locations around the perimeter of a camp. If the enemy attacked, the foo gas would be ignited from a control board within the camp, blowing hot burning liquid on the invaders.

Claymore mines were crescent shaped mines that were placed around most perimeter defenses. They were also ignited electrically. When blown, they sprayed a wide area with shrapnel because of the crescent shape. The enemy would sometimes sneak in under the wires and turn the mines around, when they attacked, the troops would spray their own positions.

Punji stakes were small slivers of bamboo, about eighteen inches in length and sharpened to a point. The small stake was placed in the ground all around a perimeter, and as close as six inches apart. The slivers were at a low angle pointed outwards towards the perimeter. Dipped in a mixture of water and water buffalo manure, they caused severe infection when slightly nicked by the point.

It was early August and hot. The special forces camp had its own airstrip which proved to be a real advantage for Captain Baker's gunship.

Because of the heat and overloaded condition of the helicopter, it did not want to come to a hover. Parking it at the end of the airstrip proved to be advantageous because a 'running take off could be managed.

By sliding the metal skids on the ground, with the use of a slight increase in collective and a forward placement of the cyclic, the helicopter would start inching forward until speed was built enough to increase the pressure on both controls to get airborne. This was a normal procedure for such conditions. And it would prove to be necessary in the Ia Drang area.

Hawk flights at Plei Me were started immediately. And, results were achieved just as quickly. The NVA had been moving into the Ia Drang in large groups without attracting the attention of the green beret contingent at Plei Me.

Captain Baker and his crew were involved in many of the firing missions during the week at Plei Me, but because of Bob's abilities, his primary function was as a chase ship for the Troop Commander.

At about the second day of the hawk flights, it became evident to the First Cavalry Division that a very large force was in the Ia Drang area, and the 2d and 3d Brigades were also brought into the action in the area.

Hawk flights were capturing and killing groups of fourteen to fifteen NVA everywhere they looked in the valley, it became so easy for the members of B Troop, it was like shooting fish in a barrel.

viii

The CBS camera, crew arrived in Plei Me on the third day of the fighting in the Ia Drang to get some coverage of the big operation. Major Barnes called Captain Baker aside and told him to take the two cameramen and the commentator along on the next hawk flight so that they could get the coverage they needed.

The gunship was really loaded. The door gunners had been left behind for this mission, but in spite of that, the two cameramen, their equipment and the reporter for CBS put a lot of extra weight in the back seat. By not refueling completely, Captain Baker figured that he could make up some of the difference in weight. Instead of the usual 1,000 pounds of fuel aboard, he was leaving Plei Me with 750 pounds.

The camera crew was positioned at each of the back doors instead of the gunners. The reporter was between the two cameramen. The reporter had a helmet on, asking questions of Captain Baker and WO1 Barrett. The questions were on the hawk flights, how many had been captured, how long the Troop had been operating in the Plei Me area and other general information. All of the radio traffic between the helicopters was being recorded when the call came from Red Charger Six.

"Red Charger SS, this is "Red Charger Six, we have a large group of NVA located at coordinates 450330, bring your passengers to that location!". "Roger Red Charger Six, will do!". Captain Baker notified the CBS crew that the enemy NVA had been located and they were headed that way.

Bob Baker shifted the large engineer map out from between the seats and ran across to 450 and then up to 350 locating the coordinates.

He stared for a few seconds at the location and then pointed to it on the map for WO1 Barrett and indicated the heading they were take.

Baker thought for a minute, then radioed. "Red Charger Six. this is Red Charger 22, over". "Red Charger 22, this is Red Charger Six, go ahead". "Roger, Red Charger Six, have you checked your charts closely?" "Roger, Red Charger 22, just bring your passengers to this location, out!".

A few minutes later, the gunship arrived at the location of the large squad of prisoners the scout ship was circling. The lift ship had arrived and the infantry blues were on the ground. The prisoners were at bay, hands on head.

The prisoners were dressed in the usual khaki uniforms of the NVA and were carrying new weapons. It was obvious that they hadn't been in country too long by their uniforms and equipment.

The camera crew and reporter from CBS indicated that they wanted to be on the ground with the troops. Captain Baker started an approach into the open area near the lift ship. Once on the ground, the cameramen and reporter joined the infantry platoon and prisoners that had been captured. Five miles inside of Laos!

ix

WO2 Jacobson returned from his scout mission with his chase ship and reported in to the operations area where he told of finding a. marshaling area with at least a hundred NVA soldiers.

Jacobson had been low level in the Ia Drang valley when he had suddenly come upon a break in the trees. There was a large lush green area beneath him with a number of NVA soldiers in different groups. One group was standing around a man in a hammock who appeared to have the soldiers rapt attention.

Jacobson did a quick pedal turn over the man in the hammock, who was laying with his hands folded behind his head, and opened fire with the twin M-60's mounted on the OH13S skids.

The men around the hammock began tailing and the hammock itself started spinning between the two small trees that supported it. Jacobson had just accounted for almost fifteen confirmed kills.

The next day, Captain Baker and his crew located one lone NVA soldier, at a trail junction, manning a .30 caliber machine gun on a tripod. Bob had been in support of one of the infantry units from the Ed Brigade during the sweeping actions that were now taking place in the Ia Drang.

Baker radioed the infantry unit commander. "Black horse 6, this is Red Charger 22, over". "This is black horse 6, go ahead Red Charger". "Roger six, we have located one NVA on a machine gun, we are presently hovering over him, do you have us in sight?" "Roger Red 22, we have you in sight and we're just a few minutes away".

Captain Baker looked out his helicopter window at the NVA soldier in the tall elephant grass beneath him. The soldier maintained his alert status at the trail junction, not offering to look up at the huge olive drab machine hovering three feet over his head.

"Door gunners, stay alert, we are going to direct the infantry in to pick this guy up, if ha even acts like he is going to elevate that machine gun, kill him!" The door gunners, rogered the instructions from Captain Baker and watched the man closely.

The lead man of the infantry unit came into sight on the trail and Captain Baker continued to move him in the direction of the aircraft. As the radio packing lead man got closer, he kept looking up at the helicopter, grinning. "Look down Black Horse, the man is right in front of you!" The radio man continued to look up at the helicopter, apparently unaware that he was within 2 to 3 feet of the enemy soldier. Finally, he got the message, looked down, and took the NVA prisoner.

The last Captain Baker saw of the NVA soldier, he was being marched off with the infantry, carrying the machine gun that he had manned at the trail junction.

xi

Major Saunders was flying in the left seat of the gunship with Lt. Wentsworth during one of the missions of the Ia Drang.

The infantry unit they were supporting came under heavy fire. The gunship was providing the close support that they required. It was Saunders first mission in one of the gunships.

Up until the flight with Wentsworth, he had been flying with the troop Commander in preparation for assuming command of the troop. Most of his time, up until now. had been in the Command and Control ship.

The .30 caliber AK-47 round came through the left window of the gunship and passed through the lower portion of Major Saunders jaw, completely removing most of his teeth and part of his tongue. The gunship crew returned Major Saunders to the medical tent where he was immediately medically evacuated to the States and Walter Reed hospital for extensive rebuilding of his lower jaw.

xii

"Captain Baker, I'm going to have a special mission for you today. We are getting a 'VIP' in to observe the operations in the Ia Drang. He is flying in to Pleiku today and will be arriving here by helicopter". "I'll want you to stay with him all day, give him anything he wants, then return him to Pleiku, this evening".

When Baker asked who the man was, the reply was, "I don't know anything other than to give him the very best treatment, VIP status!".

The man that arrived early in the morning was wearing a black patch over one eye and had an oriental camera man with him. He was very interested in the operation and wanted to spend as much time as possible over the battle area, observing the action. During the returns to the special forces camp for re-armament or fuel, the man and his camera man were looking at captured materials.; NVA and asking a. lot of questions.

At the end of the day, Captain Baker returned the VIP to the helicopter pad at Pleiku and shook his hand and saluted. Bob would find out a few years later that he had spent the day with Moshe Dyan.

Although he was a VIP in 1966, General Dyan did not make his name a household word until June of 1967 during the 'six day war' when Israel took the Gaza strip and occupied the Sinai peninsula.

The Ia Drang. Plei Me actions lasted about as long as the six day war. At the end of the battle in August of 1966, B Troop had distinguished itself again with credit for a large number of the 861 enemy soldiers killed in the action. The Troop was awarded the Valorous Unit Citation for the action. The same award as a silver star for each individual.

CHAPTER FOUR

RAIN, RAIN AND more rain. It had reached it's peak as the Troop set up operations in the Bong Son area, in preparation for operation Irving. It was a constant, it never stopped!

Captain Baker and his crew had been involved in a support mission for one of the Division brigades. During the mission they managed to capture a Chinese made AK-47 machine gun. It immediately became barter material for better things.

B Troop set up it's campsite on the outskirts of a new Air Force base, still under construction. The base was near a village called Phu Cat. As soon as the troop was in place, Major Barnes was informed that hot showers, an officer's club and a PX, were available to the members of the troop. The troop commander declined the offer for any of the facilities for the troops and officers, He felt the troops "might make the 1/3th look bad".

The troop commander even decided that the PX was off limits to the troops. "One individual could be selected to buy for everyone in the platoon". Although he admired the troop commander, Captain Baker disagreed with him on his decision regarding the facilities.

Baker also decided that other ways of getting better living conditions might be available through bartering of the captured enemy guns or other captured items, such as flags.

All of the officers and men of the troop were living under miserable conditions, and had been for the six months that Captain Baker had been a member. The tents leaked constantly, the food was poor most of the time, and they lived by candlelight at night. None of them had been able to take a decent bath in months.

Members of the Air Force were beginning to find their way to the troop area. They wanted to see these strange beings from the Army that were unclean, ate C rations, and were at their best, only when they were killing the enemy.

ii

Captain Baker discover the solution to the problem in one Sergeant First Class in the Air Force. And a supply sergeant at that.

Air Force SFC Larry Matic had wandered into the troop area to look it over just like the other spectators. Larry was an avid student of weapons and was extremely interested in the weapons systems on the gunships.

Larry's genuine interest and desires to know more about this ragtag outfit led to a friendship with Captain Baker that was to last for months. It was not a friendship of necessity, but one based on mutual respect. Baker had been enlisted once, and had not forgotten.

SFC Matic was keenly interested in the captured AK-47 machine gun. He mentioned that the Air Base commander had been looking for one that could be displayed on the wall of the 'officer's club'. A bargain was struck immediately. Captain Baker gave the machine gun to Larry Matic, who in turn presented it to the base commander. With Captain Baker's compliments.

Soon, the word came back from the base commander to "give Captain Baker anything he wanted, as long as it could be accounted for, or had no serial numbers".

Tents were the first thing that Captain Baker asked for. The Air Force had the standard GP (general purpose) tents available to them, and they were not going to be used. All of the buildings at the new air base were permanent construction. The GP tent was large, waterproof, high enough that you didn't have to walk into it stoop shouldered, and it housed a dozen or more people.

Within the day, 2 five ton trucks arrived in the Troop area and a contingent of Air Force enlisted men unloaded the tents. The tents were erected where the platoon leaders wanted the troops to be. It was to be the first time in over four months, that everyone was going to sleep in a dry bed.

Prior to the GP tents, each platoon was laid out within the confines of the troop area. The hex tents would house E people. Three when crowded. The tents leaked, blew down easily when the helicopters hovered near them.

Shortly after the GP tents were delivered, SFC Larry Matic approached Captain Baker about a. ride in the gunship. The request presented no problem for Captain Baker or the crew. A door gunner would be replaced by SFC Matic whenever the Air Force sergeant was available. And, the door gunner would get some much needed rest.

During the first mission., with SFC Matic on the door gun, the troop got into some heavy enemy activity. Matic killed over ten of the enemy in one day. He told Captain Baker that he spent over sixteen years in the Air Force and always wanted to be more involved, but had been buried in the supply system. He finally had his dreams come true in the battle area with another military service.

Within a day or so, another group of Air Force enlisted personnel arrived in the troop area with materials and tools. To the amazement of all, they constructed shower stalls replete with shower heads, faucets and soap dishes. The water supply was provided by above the ground plastic pipes tapped into the water supply at the air base. Baker thought, "The wind must have been blowing their way!"

Baker decided to broaden his barter capability. Flags were the answer. There was one problem, Baker hadn't seen many enemy flags, let alone capture one. It was going to be necessary to have some made.

One of the local villages had a repair shop. Baker made contact and asked them to produce a few NVA flags. Although they agreed, for the right price, the civilians were nervous about making them, they were afraid the RVN soldiers might stumble onto the flags while they were being sewn.

Once the flags were made, they were left in a mud hole overnight to age them. The painful part was the blood spots that were needed. Baker had to prick his finger to get the blood.

SFC Matic showed up for another tour as door gunner. He had noticed that Captain Baker didn't have any weapon with him when he went on a mission other than the issue .38 special revolver. "I had this M3 carbine that I thought you might like to have when you are on missions". The carbine was a WWII issue with the automatic selector and 30 round banana clips. A 500 round box of ammunition was also provided.

The ammunition fit snugly under the front seat of the gunship, the carbine was slung over the armor plate of the seat.

iii

Lt. Wentsworth'5 co-pilot reported to Captain Baker that the lieutenant was beginning to act strangely. Baker wasn't surprised. Lately, the lieutenant had been threatening to fly under the bridge that spanned the river north of the Phu Cat laager area.

Captain Jim Higgins, the lift platoon leader, had also mentioned a few days earlier that Lt. Wentsworth was getting his preparation fire (rocket fire into a landing zone to discourage enemy fire) in too close when the lift aircraft were landing into an assault area.

Captain Baker talked to Lt. Wentsworth about his flying and the Lieutenant had seemed unconcerned about the criticism. On the point of the flight under the bridge, he had said, "It's there, and if I want to fly under it, I will!" Captain Baker said, "that is an order, get the bridge out of your mind!".

iv

The hawk flight was just south of Phu Cat. Major Barnes was watching over the mission. He had requested Captain Baker for his chase. The area near the lift ships had been 'prepped' by Captain Baker's 2.75" rockets. The troops were on the ground, with a scout ship above them. The gunship was overhead to provide support, if needed.

Thirty minutes into the mission, there was a loud 'Boom' in the rear of Baker's aircraft. Baker looked at his instruments and noticed he was beginning to lose power. The aircraft was also getting a temperature rise on the exhaust gas temperature gauge. Although autorotations were never a problem for Baker, he wasn't fond of the idea, in a heavy gunship. He had not expended enough fuel or armament.

"Red Charger Six, we have taken a bad hit in the engine area". "We are looking for a place to put it down." Captain Baker looked at the open spots available. One field looked possible for an autorotation. but it was shoulder to shoulder with what appeared to be Vietnamese farmers, all raking the same small area.

Baker decided not to take a chance on the people actually being farmers and started the trip back to Phu Cat. Being captured was not one of Baker's favorite topics. He had heard the stories of the pilots who were shot down and captured, prior to his arrival.

They had found one of them later, hanging from a tree, skinned alive. And, since that time B Troop had become well known in country. All of the gunship pilots had a 5,000 dollar price tag on their heads, by name.

The chances of getting the aircraft safely back to the laager area was slim. But still, it was a better risk than putting it down in a questionable area. Baker hadn't run out of skill or ideas yet!

Fortunately, it was a short trip back. Not more than ten or fifteen minutes of flying time. The aircraft was set up for a normal approach, All of the crew members were holding their breaths while the aircraft engine gauges showed the needles rode the red lines. The aircraft touched down and the engine was shut down immediately.

Billy Garner was waiting for Bob's return after he heard the call that Baker's aircraft had been hit in the engine. On short final, the engine was coming apart. It was beginning to spit large red hot pieces, "as big as softballs", out of the tail pipe. The aircraft had been hit dead center in the compressor section of the big jet engine and was literally chewing itself up on the way home.

V

Captain Garner contacted Baker as soon as he landed after a short flight back to An Khe to pick up some materials needed from the rear area. "I want you to look at Wentworth's aircraft, the whole damn front of the aircraft is blown out!".

The two chin bubbles were both out of the lower part of the aircraft and the aluminum nose of the ship looked like a sieve. From the appearance of the damage, it was evident that the Lieutenant had been too close to his target. He had blown the front of the helicopter all to hell with his own 40 mm shrapnel.

Captain Baker began chewing Lt. Wentsworth up one side and down the other. The lieutenant listened. then saluted and walked off to his tent. After Wentsworth had gone. Baker was looking at the helicopter when the crew chief approached him and said, "You should have seen it Captain, the lieutenant sure saved their asses!". Baker said, "Tell me about it Sergeant!"

Lt. Wentsworth was in the area west of Phu Cat when he received a call from an infantry unit pinned down by a heavy machine gun in a bunker. They had two wounded men between them and the bunker, and could not get to the men because of the machine gun fire.

Lt. Wentsworth had tried conventional methods of putting the machine gun position out of action, with rocket fire and then 40 mm fire. The bunker was in a small hill with the gun firing out of a small aperture. No matter what was tried, the crew could not get a. round into the small opening. In the meantime., the wounded men were lying on the ground, slowly bleeding to death.

Wentsworth and his crew tried it from all angles and finally, out of exasperation, they hovered the aircraft off to one side of the hill, just out of view. Suddenly, they moved sideways into position, stuffed the barrel of the 40mm gun into the aperture and pulled the trigger.

vi

SFC Matic was becoming, a familiar face to all of the men of B Troop, In fact, he was beginning to become one of the troopers. Since the arrival of the tents, the entire troop received pillows, new blankets, wash pans for bathing and shaving and many other items.

During one of his trips to fly door gunner, Matic asked why the troop didn't have a generator for electricity in the tents. When told that the troop was only authorized one 1.5 kilowatt generator for the radios, he offered to get a generator that had just arrived with the "new ice cream machine". Since the air base had it's own central power unit, the generator for the ice cream machine wasn't needed.

The generator and all of the necessary wiring, sockets and bulbs were delivered the next day, by nightfall each GP tent had electric lights.

Baker had not missed the statement, "ice cream machine". They had to be kidding! The troop had not seen ice cream since he had been with them, and here was an ice cream machine, almost within Baker's grasp!

This was the only time that the Troop Commander and Baker had agreed on anything. They both had a mutual love for ice cream. That afternoon. Baker took the troop commanders jeep and started the short journey into the land of OZ, the air base.

The Air Force cook was a Sergeant First Class. Yes, he understood the problem, but no, he couldn't do anything about it. Yes, he would sure as hell like to have a captured NVA flag or SKS rifle, but he still couldn't do anything about it.

The cook's problem was that he had the machinery for the ice cream, but he didn't have any ice cream mix. Baker asked, "What if I get the ice cream mix?". The sergeant quickly answered, "If you get the ice cream mix, we will give you one gallon for each two gallons of mix".

"Major Barnes, if you will let me borrow one of the lift helicopters for a. couple of days, I will locate the ice cream mix back at An Khe." "If we can find the mix, we can have ice cream the rest of the time we are in the Phu Cat area." This is the first time Captain Baker had seen Major Barnes turn glassy eyed.

vii

The flight to An Khe was only 15 minutes from the temporary troop area at Phu Cat, The road between the Bong Son area and An Khe was secure and heavily traveled with military trucks.

The problem after landing, was transportation to the Division area and the store house of ice cream mix. Baker almost had sugar plums dancing in his head. Here was a chance to provide something special for the troops and also a chance to do what he did best. Getting what he wanted! His background as a navy enlisted man had to pay off.

The transportation problem proved frustrating each time it was necessary to go to An Khe. The small contingent of personnel in the rear area had the few vehicles available and always managed to have them tied up for one reason or another.

Hitch hiking was the easiest way to get from one place to another. Usually that was the only way because of the vehicle shortage. Baker decided to try the thumb.

The first jeep stopped to pick up Baker. The driver was a SP4, and the passenger was a Major from the First Cavalry Division. The Major asked, "where are you going captain?" Captain Baker explained that he was trying to get to the Division supply area, in a search for ice cream mix.

The Major shifted his opulent body and turned around to face Baker riding in the back of the jeep and said, "What do you want ice cream mix for?". Baker answered, "To make ice cream!" The Major twisted the toothpick around in his mouth, furrowed his brow and said, "What do you want to make ice cream for?", "we're getting plenty of that in the Division!" Baker remained silent the rest of the trip.

After several attempts to locate ice cream mix in the Division area, Captain Baker returned to the UHID lift ship at the Golf Course and flew back to Phu Cat. He had at least accomplished something.

During one of his conversations with the supply people, Baker had discovered that all of the supplies for II Corps were routed out of the depot at Qui Nhon. The question still remained, whether or not the ice cream mix was available.

The next day, the lift ship was pre-flighted and lifted off for Captain Baker's foray into the mammoth supply system at Qui Nhon. The trip took less than 30 minutes to the landing area closest to the large supply facility

Captain Baker put his thumb out again and asked directions to the supply depot. After a few minutes, he was at the gate, and possible success.

Baker walked up to the gate and was stopped by a military policeman who said, "sorry Captain, you can't get in without a pass." This was beginning to get discouraging. After a few minutes of trying to convince the MP that he had forgotten his pass, that it was swept away during the last monsoon and that it was destroyed in a mortar attack, Captain Baker turned away and started back the way he came.

While walking back towards the helicopter, a jeep passed him. As Baker watched the jeep, it was quickly waived through the gate by the MP who wouldn't believe the most logical of stories.

Baker stopped for a moment and sat down on a large rock. As he watched, he began to notice that the vehicles gaining access to the supply facility had a blue identification ticket in the lower right corner of the windshield.

Captain Baker returned to the helicopter and retrieved a clipboard and some loose papers that he had noticed in the aircraft. He then started back towards the supply depot. Around a bend, and just out of sight of the gate guard, he waited. As soon as he heard a vehicle coming, he looked for the blue identification sticker. Finally, a jeep appeared, blue sticker and all. Captain Baker stuck his thumb out.

The civilian driver said, "where are you going Captain?" Baker said, "My jeep broke down a few blocks back and I'm running late for a meeting at the depot!"

As the jeep passed through the gate, Captain Baker returned the MP's salute and gave him a polite wave. Once inside, it was just a matter of finding what he needed.

The civilian operating the fork lift saw the Captain with the clip board and asked, "what are you looking for Captain?" Baker answered, "ice cream mix." The civilian motioned for the Captain to follow him and took him around to the next tier of buildings and pointed, "right there Captain, how many do you want?"

"One hundred boxes is all we need right now!" The civilian looked at Baker and said, "I sure as hell hate to break these pallets down, they have 200 boxes on them and we can't get rid of this damned stuff as it is!"

As soon as the fork lift had the pallet out of the storage shed, Captain Baker explained that his truck had broken down just outside the gate and he needed assistance getting it to the landing pad. "If you could transport it to the airfield, I'll do you a favor and take 200 boxes off of your hands!"

The civilian truck driver and helper plus the crew loaded the ice cream mix in the lift ship. After the last box was in Captain Baker thanked the supply personnel for all of their help and started the return trip to Phu Cat.

Major Barnes couldn't believe it. That night, the mess tent had strawberry ice cream. The following night they had chocolate, then vanilla, then pecan. The Air Force ice cream machine had finally been put to good use.

There was one negative result from the 'ice cream caper'. The 1/9th squadron commander was presented with a dish of ice cream from Major Barnes along with the story of how it had been obtained.

The Colonel had turned to his supply officer, Major Nathan Dredd, and said, "Baker should be my supply officer, not you!". Major Dredd was to become the new B Troop commander, and Captain Baker's superior, within weeks.

viii

The Vietnamese village of Phu Cat adjoined the new air base under construction, The village residents had been moved out by the South Vietnamese government because of the construction of the new air field. The village was virtually abandoned, except for some enemy activity that took place under the cover of darkness.

The air base perimeter was well marked with signs, The fence line itself consisted of coils of barbed wire and concertina wire (flat metal coils with razor sharp edges).

Although the Air Force Police patrolled the perimeter surrounding the air base. B Troop provided assistance on a daily basis by flying first light and last light missions around the perimeter. The missions were flown to look for evidence of penetration, or the enemy.

During many off the B Troop missions, potential sappers (NVA carrying a satchel charge of TNT) were killed while attempting to breach the wire of the perimeter.

Whenever a. kill was confirmed, it delighted the air base commander because he knew that it discouraged additional attempts. But, it upset the Air Force air police commander. The air police commander felt that it was an indication that he wasn't doing his job. The more it upset the captain, the harder Captain Baker and the rest of the gunship pilots looked for sappers.

During several of the missions, Captain Baker and Captain Billy Garner would team up as pilot and co-pilot. Billy had been wanting to fly on the combat missions more and more often. He was also becoming very intrigued by the village of Phu Cat. "I wonder if there is anything in there of value?"

When Billy couldn't stand it any longer, he took a helicopter outside the perimeter and landed in the village to make a quick trip through several of the thatch roofed hooches. Billy paused only long enough to grab a small bed out of one of the hooches close to he aircraft.

The bed was light weight, made of bamboo and tied together with rope cross members to support a mattress. Billy returned to the troop area with his new "Z machine", and often would announce to Baker. "I can just hear my Z machine beckoning me!".

Billy couldn't get the village out of his mind. Whenever he could, he would broach the subject with Captain Baker. "There is all sorts of stuff in there, I saw brass chimes and a. Buddha in one of the places". Finally, the fever hit Baker too. Plans were made for a quick incursion into the abandoned village.

Two of the small OH13S helicopter were borrowed by Billy and Captain Baker. Two volunteer observers and the two captains made the trip into the village.

The small helicopters were landed just outside of the village. The collective pitch controls were locked in the down position and the engines left running in case a. quick lift off was necessary.

The two captains and the two enlisted men ran in and out of hooches looking for plunder. All four were armed to the teeth with M-15's and hand grenades. The Buddha, chimes and several other small items were removed and returned quickly to the copters.

The Buddha became barter for Captain Garner. He met an Air Force captain at the new air base that was interested in owning anything military or Vietnamese. The Buddha was a prize possession.

After the trade was complete, the Air Force captain put the Buddha outside of his room in the officer's area of the air base. He would return to his room at night, after a few at the officer's club, place his steel pot on top of the Buddha's bald head and retire.

The air base was nearing completion. Some of the menial tasks, such as laundry, sweeping and cleaning were being contracted out to the local civilian populace, Each morning, before sunrise, the civilians that had been hired would be ushered into the front gate and assigned their duties under the watchful eyes of air policemen.

The proud owner of the Buddha had just completed his shower and shave and put on his air force work uniform for the day. As he stepped out of the door of his room, he found fifteen prostrate Vietnamese in front of the Buddha. The Buddha was wearing his steel pot!

It took a little doing, but the Air Force captain managed to get a room change that afternoon. For some reason, sleeping in that same room again, hid ho appeal

ix

The gunships of the troop were being assigned search and destroy missions in the Bonb Son area. More and more hits were taken in the aircraft. It was evidence there was a lot of enemy activity in the plains.

Captain Baker, his co-pilot Barrett, the crew chief and door gunner were north of the Bong Son area checking out the trails, streams and villages when they caught sight of four NVA starting across a shallow stream.

Captain Baker fired one pair of 2.75" rockets, killing one NVA in the middle of the Stream. The other three made it across the stream and into the thick underbrush surrounding a rice paddy.

Baker hovered the aircraft around the bank of the paddy looking for the three NVA. As each one was located, he would point them out to the door gunners and tell them to fire.

After the three were located and killed, Captain Baker received a radio call, "Red Charger 22, this is Red Charger 5, I want to see you in my tent as soon as you return to the troop area!"

Captain Baker saluted Major Barnes as he entered his tent. "You told me to report to you sir!" "God damn it Baker, what are you trying to do?", "I just decided to get out into the area to observe the action, and what do I see?" "Your down hovering around killing dinks arid you haven't made the required calls for clearance to fire!"

Captain Baker then told the Major about his first incident when the NVA managed to get to the spider hole before a round could be fired.

"Major Barnes, I came over here to do a job, which I feel that I am doing!" "If you feel that I am doing it wrong, I won't squeeze another trigger!".

Major Barnes looked at the Captain for a minute and then said, "Look Bob, I know you're doing what is right, just be careful!".

SP4 Barney had been in country nearly nine months. He had been assigned as a technician with the maintenance crews and worked directly for Captain Garner. If a part had to be acquired in order to get a helicopter back in the air, SP4 Barney could get it sooner than any of his peers.

Barney had been in college studying to become a dentist when he was drafted and sent to South Viet Nam. He had weathered it well. In fact, he had enjoyed his assignment enough to reenlist in the Army for another six years. Because he was a technician, the reenlistment provided him a special bonus of nearly 12,000 dollars.

Shortly after his reenlistment, Barney applied for Officer's Candidate School and had been accepted. He would return to the United States in 30 days and attend DCS. Once the schooling was completed, Barney would be richer by 12,000 dollars, a second lieutenant and have only three years obligation as an officer!

Before leaving South Viet Name Barney decided that he would like to go out with the infantry on one search and destroy mission.

The infantry blues were out on the search and destroy mission north of Bong Son, Barney was close to the point man for the mission when he stepped on the mine. Barney lost his right foot on the only infantry mission of his career.

xi

Lt. Wentsworth replaced his door gunner with the Air Force flight surgeon. The doctor had arrived in the troop area asking to go on one of the missions in the Bong Son area.

Up until this time, there had been no problems with any of the Air Force replacements for the door gunners position. SFC Matic had been flying missions on a regular basis with Captain Baker and had been awarded an air medal. The word got out about the type of flying that B Troop did, and there were plenty of volunteers.

The doctor received his instruction on the M-60 machine gun and was provided with a helmet and told all of the commands from the front seat, when to shoot, and when not to shoot.

The search and destroy missions were continuing in the area to the north of Bong Son, and the fire from the ground was getting heavier each day. The enemy was making preparations for something big, and they were very active.

The NVA didn't hesitate to fire at Wentsworth's helicopter. The rounds riddled the left side of the aircraft from the nose to the tail rotor. The doctor had been assigned to the left side. One of the rounds from the .30 caliber AK-47 entered the rear door gunner area and struck the doctor dead center between the eyes.

The next day, the orders were out. No more replacements for the door gunners. The order also included SFC Matic. SFC Matic was beginning to catch some flack from the Air Force. His superiors felt that he was spending too much time with B Troop, and not enough time with his own job in the supply room.

The Air Force police captain had initiated an investigation into all of the property that had disappeared from the Air Force property rooms, only to end up in B Troop. Although he was not guilty of any wrongdoing, SFC Matic was soon transferred out of South Viet Nam to Korea.

From that day on, Captain Baker made it a point to find more and more NVA getting through the air force wire perimeter, When the enemy was found in the wire, Baker made a direct report of the kills to the air base commander.

xii

The Soui Ca Valley was a few 'clicks' north of Bong Son and set back into the hills to the west of the Bong Son plains. Because of the increased enemy activity, it seemed like a. good place for hawk flights.

The hawk flight started early that morning with the blues on the ground, covered by one scout ship, Captain Baker's gunship and Major Barnes in the command and control aircraft.

The blues had just been inserted in the entrance of the valley and the lift ship departed to await orders for the extraction. The scout ship was hovering over the blues as they began to search a trail network.

Major Barnes called Captain Baker, "Red 22. this is Red Charger Six", "stay with the blues for a while, I'm going to look around the valley!" Baker stayed over the infantry and the scout ship, watching for any indication of problems when the call carne out that was to result in a ten hour flying day for Baker.

"Red 22, Red 22, I'm just a little north of you and I have a company in the open!" "Get over here quick!" Baker made a right turn and saw Major Barnes's helicopter. Machine gun fire was coming from the door gunners positions and being directed into a dry creek bed not more than 1,000 meters away from Baker's location.

As soon as Baker and his crew arrived, the dry creek bed revealed a company size unit of NVA soldiers diving for cover, They had been marching in the creek bed which had 15 foot sheer walls on each side. There was no place to go. and they were in the open. WO Barrett lined up the gunship with the creek bed that ran east and west in the Soui Ca valley and Baker lined up the 40mm grenade on the fleeing NVA, and squeezed the trigger.

The enemy unit started diving for any cover they could find as the 40 mm grenades began exploding in their ranks.

It appeared to Baker that the black puffs of exploding grenades split the middle of the fleeing ranks of NVA. Those on the left dived towards a washed out crevice at the bottom of the dried out stream bed and those on the right chose the same cover on their side.

By the time the first 40mm run was complete, the enemy had managed to get into the crevices. The crevices did not offer complete cover for the NVA. Each one of the enemy soldiers had a small portion of their bodies still exposed to the aircraft overhead.

Major Barnes had already completed a radio call to the rear laager area in Bong Son and the rest of the gunships, lift ships and infantry blues were enroute to the valley.

Captain Baker finished the first run and started around a second time with the 40mm trying to get some of the exploding grenades in close to the crevice on each side of the sheer wall. On the third run, the gunships from the troop began arriving.

The troop set up a daisy chain of gunships hovering slowly along the top part of the bank of the creek bed. door gunners were used to spray the portions of the NVA still visible to them. Captain Baker was pitching hand grenades out the window, trying to roll them into the crevice with the NVA soldiers.

After the first hour of action, lift ships began putting infantry on the ground for the mopping up portion, while scouts and gunships formed into 'pink teams' (one red gunship and one white scout) to continue locating pockets of enemy resistance.

The troop had managed to trap the NVA 30th Engineer Regiment in the valley. The regiment had been caught flat footed and totally unprepared for the devastation that B Troop dumped on them during that one day. A captured NVA lieutenant stated during interrogation later that, during the briefing in North Viet Nam, they had been told. "Don't worry about the helicopters down south".

The NVA remained in a daze that day. The soldiers would be found in small groups of two to three, attempting to find someplace to hide. Sometimes, because of the shock of what had happened, they just stayed put.

Captain Baker and his crew found one NVA crouching under a bush, holding a. captured Thompson sub machine gun across his lap. The gunship was at a hover when the pair of 2.75" rockets were fired almost point blank into the lap of the solider. When the smoke had cleared, he was gone.

Throughout the day, small pockets of NVA were found in a. daze wandering around in the valley. If they didn't throw down their weapons, they were killed. Those that showed signs of surrendering were airlifted out of the huge battle area.

While hovering around in the area, Captain Baker's crew found knapsacks hanging from the limbs of the trees in a small lightly wooded area. The gunship landed and the gunner dismounted and removed the knapsacks of medical supplies from what had been the regimental medical area.

Lt. Wentsworth and his gunship crew found one NVA who didn't want to surrender: Wentsworth was at a hover and much too close when he fired his pair of rockets. He was so close that the rocket did not have a chance to arm the point detonating warhead. Instead, it skewered the NVA where he stood.

xiii

During one of the return flights for rearming and refueling, Billy Garner joined Captain Baker for the next mission while WO Barrett rested and ate. The had just returned to the Soui Ca, when one of the scout ships called.

"Red 22, this is white 12, we are to the north of the main battle area and we are receiving fire from a hooch!" "Roger white 12, we're on the way!". The hooch was situated in the northern neck of the valley. It was similar in appearance to an adobe house, with a thatch roof.

White 12, marked the hooch with smoke and laid off to the south, out of the way, Billy said, "Let me give it a try with the rockets".

The first run towards the hooch, when the pair of rockets were fired, was not successful, The rockets swooshed out of the tubes and went wide to the left. The second run was attempted at a different angle, and went over the hooch. After the third try. Billy said, "I can't hit the damned thing, see what you can do".

Baker took the controls and repeated the run towards the front of the hooch. The left seat of the UH1 gunship did not have a sighting device for rockets, but Baker had learned through experience that he could get some degree of accuracy by using the whip antenna mounted on the nose of the aircraft. The tip of the antenna had a six inch yellow tip, When the bottom part of the yellow tip was put on the target, Baker had been able to achieve some degree of accuracy.

Baker slowly lined the gunship up and made sure that he wasn't adding any collective (which had a tendency to make the rockets veer upward), he steadied the ship, lined up the lower part of the yellow tip of the antenna directly on the open door of the hooch, and pressed the button.

"Swoooosh" The pair of rockets left the launchers and started towards the hooch. Baker and Garner watched, awe struck, as the pair of rockets entered the open front door, without pausing to ring the doorbell.

There were twin booms of the rockets, and then a. tremendous secondary explosion as the rockets ignited the hooch full of enemy munitions.

The hooch had apparently been the storehouse for the regiments ammunition and explosives. The two captains watched the slow motion scence, as the thatch roof slowly left the hooch to fifteen feet in the air, then as the walls caved inward, the thatch roof slowly settled down on the rubble.

xiv

Captain Higgens was putting the squad of infantry into the landing zone in the Soui Ca. valley. As the right skid touched the ground, Jim noticed that the aircraft was still settling on the left side. The door gunner called the Captain on the intercom and said, "Sir, you're on a slope!" Jim acknowledged the call and added a little right cyclic into the direction of the right skid to hold the aircraft against the slope as he continued down with the collective control.

"Sir, you're still on the slope!". Higgens again acknowledged the door gunner on the intercom and continued the downward pressure of the collective, waiting for the left skid to touch.

Higgens had been good on slope landings in flight school, and this one wasn't any more difficult than the slopes in the training areas in Alabama. Learning how to land a. helicopter, on the side of a hill, or slope, was probably the hardest part of all of the training, If a heavy helicopter is put down on a slight incline, the metal skids will slide, and the helicopter can roll over.

By applying cyclic towards the slope and at the same time gently reducing collective pitch in the blades, the helicopter can be safely put on the ground. The pilot continues to work the skid into the slope putting the weight where it will prevent a slide. Higgens was applying the school solution.

Higgens felt the left skid touch down, and the door gunner on the left confirmed, on the intercom, that he had firm contact with the ground. The right door gunner again said, "Sir, you're still on the slope, but I think he's dead now!" Higgens had firmly planted the right skid of the ton and a half of aluminum, fuel and passengers right on top of a hiding NVA soldier.

XV

That same day Billy and Captain Baker were flying in support of one of the Division infantry units which had been air lifted into the valley.

Billy had still not gotten over the luck of the two rockets going in the front door of the hooch and was hoping for a chance to redeem himself.

The infantry unit called Baker's guns-hip while the gunship team was in their area. "Red 22, this is Lone Star 5, we have a badly wounded man, he has to be medically evacuated, can you help us?"

Bob Baker and Billy discussed the situation, and very quickly decided to attempt the evacuation in the gunship. Because of all of the activity in the valley, the lift ships were not readily available.

The U.S. unit popped red smoke (the standard signal for wounded) and the two captains looked for the landing zone, The landing zone was directly in the midst of the infantry unit receiving fire. It was on the edge of a small stream and in a. very small opening. Almost too small for the gunship.

As the gunship sat down on the skids, the infantry brought the wounded man to the helicopter for extraction to the medical unit. The soldier had caught a. round directly in the middle of his forehead. As he coughed, gray matter and blood spurted from the opening in the back of his head.

Once the man was loaded, the heavy gunship was eased out of the small clearing backwards and then pedal turned around for takeoff. All of this time, the infantry was receiving fire, but no rounds reached the helicopter. The infantry soldier died en route to the medical unit.

CHAPTER FIVE

OPERATIONS IRVING AND Thayer II continued from early October 1966 through February of 1967, The operations were along the south China Sea Coast and the Bong Son plains in Binh Dinh Province.

Bong Son had been a. constant problem as long as Captain Baker had been with B Troop, There were continuing stories of the actions that had taken place in the Bong Son plains prior to his arrival. After nearly a year, it continued to be an enemy stronghold.

The year of the horse would be be corning to a close in the latter part of January 1967. At that time, the Vietnamese celebrated TET, and the beginning of the year of the sheep.

Up until now, the First Cavalry Division had been very successful. Many of the troops within the division felt that a part of the success may have been related to the suspicious nature of the Vietnamese during the year of the horse. The first cavalry emblem is the head of a horse over a wide diagonal bar.

The infantry troops had taken advantage of the suspicious nature of the Vietnamese in the jungle areas. When a kill was made, the troops had begun placing the 1st Cavalry patch on the body of the dead enemy soldier.

If the body was in a trench area, the troops Placed the patch on the body and also slipped a grenade under the dead soldier with the pin pulled.

The lever held the grenade in a safe position until the body was moved. Sometimes, the U.S. troops were still close enough to hear the NVA scrambling to climb the walls of the hole, in an attempt to get out after they had heard the distinct 'pop' of the fuze igniter on the grenade while trying to move their comrade.

ii

The heavy concentration of enemy in the Bong Son area was still evident. Captain Baker, his co-pilot WO1 Barrett, the door gunner and crew chief just lifted off from the Troop pad at LZ English. Heading north, at low level, along highway 1 they received a long burst of AK47 machine gun fire from the right side. Several hits were experienced immediately.

Although the gunship is noisy, the crew helmets filtered a lot of outside noise, permitting good radio communications at the same time. One noise that was not filtered out was fire directed at the aircraft. It had a very special sound to it.

The crack of the rifle, or the sharp staccato of the machine guns was always very different from the noise of a fire fight that was off in the distance. When the rounds had your name on them, you knew it immediately. Baker experienced enough fire through the cockpit to be very familiar with the sound, and these had been close enough to smell and taste. When the fire was close, Baker could actually smell the nitrates.

Baker immediately banked left and lost a. few feet of the altitude that he had to spare, leveling off just above the trees. The attempt to get away from the fire on the right was futile. Another long burst of machine gun fire now started from the left. No matter which way he turned, the aircraft was in it. The rounds were entering the aircraft from both sides.

"Crack", the round came through the front of the aircraft. WO I Barret jerked, and said, "I'm hit!". Baker looked at him and didn't see any evidence of any severe damage except for a small trickle of blood coming from his lower lip.

The round had entered through the front of the aircraft. It struck the instrument panel in front of the right seat of the helicopter and then plowed through the top of the cyclic stick. The .30 caliber round then ricocheted up into WO I Barrett's chicken plate, where it stopped, just a half an inch below the top of the armor and Barrett's throat. Parts consisting of buttons, screws and plastic hit Barrett in the mouth causing a. small laceration.

WO I Barrett was deposited at the medical tent and the aircraft returned to the Troop laager area to survey the damage. The top of the cyclic stick had been blown off. Where there had once been an array of buttons that controlled the intercom, transmitter switch and firing buttons, nothing remained except the wires which were splayed up and exposed.

Only 59 days left! Baker had gone through a. transition of accepting the possibilities of dying in combat to the realization that he was now down to less than 2 months with rotation to the U.S., and safety. He was now beginning to spend most of his spare time filling sand bags around his sleeping area in an effort to provide safety at night. But getting through the day time missions was becoming more difficult!

Major Nathan Dredd had taken over as Troop commander within the past few weeks. Unlike Barnes, who was tough, Major Dredd sat around the operations tent with his head in his hands. Dredd didn't care for Baker, the Captain who had made him look bad during the ice cream incident.

During his first six months with the 1/9th, Major Dredd had been assigned to staff duties. These duties managed to keep him in the rear area and away from any threat of danger. The word was out in the Troop that Major Dredd logged several hundred hours of combat flying time during the six months. A difficult thing to do, when not in combat.

"Captain, how soon can you get back into the air?" "You're needed out in the AD (Area. Operations) as soon as possible!". Captain Baker showed the cyclic stick wires to the Troop Commander, only to be told, "That isn't critical, get it back into the air!".

Baker left the aircraft to locate Captain Billy Garner. "Take a. look at the cyclic on the aircraft and ground it if you can!" Billy readily agreed and grounded the aircraft from further flight until the bare wires could be fixed. Baker had said, "If this aircraft isn't grounded, and I start it up, I hope the wires short out and a rocket is fired right up that dumb bastards ass!".

Meanwhile, Dredd sat in the operations tent, with his head in his hands

iii

The infantry unit was in a. heavily wooded area, and receiving fire from across the river which adjoined the woods. The infantry commander had contacted Captain Baker and his new co-pilot WO2 Richley.

Richley had been working in maintenance with Captain Billy Garner and volunteered to get back into the gunships, specifically asking to fly with Baker. Baker felt that he must be suicidal because "none of the other pilots wanted to fly co-pilot in his aircraft!

Checking along the river banks at low level was the normal way to locate the NVA. Usually, they fired at the helicopters, giving their position away. The crew had checked the river banks several times with no success. The infantry commander was adamant, his unit was still receiving fire.

A small village was on the other side of the river. It had a heavily wooded area on the north side. The gunship crew finally located the source of the infantry's problem in a long trench dug along the edge of the wooded area. The trench was perpendicular to the river, offering a wide field of fire for the three NVA occupying it. They were able to rise up out of the trench and fire bursts of machine gun fire at the troops across the river with little or no exposure time.

Captain Baker told Richley. "Hold the aircraft at a hover!". The gunship was positioned over the friendly troops on one side of the river, the nose of the aircraft lined up with the trench on the other side. Baker methodically took the 40mm gun sight down from it's overhead position and lined the sight up on the three NVA in the trench.

By this time, the three NVA soldiers were scrambling for a place to hide. They had a choice of climbing out of the trench into the open area, or they could run the length of the trench in an attempt to get away from the exploding grenades that were beginning to join them.

Baker continued firing, long, then short, long then short. The three NVA were running back and forth in the trench line trying to outrun the grenades. The grenades finally caught them midway during the run back and forth.

During this time, another NVA soldier was taking careful aim on the stationary target with his AK47. Another three hits, and another slight wound for the new co-pilot.

Once the mission was completed, the gunship headed back to assess the damage. WOS Rich ley had sustained a very minor wound, but decided to stick it out with Baker the rest of his tour. Baker was now convinced that Richley was mad.

iv

The Crescent area was north of LZ English. It was bordered by mountains on the north and south, the highway on the west and the South China Sea on the east.

The Crescent area, was known to be a large enemy stronghold, The operation into this area would be comprised of soldiers from S. Korea, South Vietnam and the U.S.

The multi-national forces began the push from the highway and the mountains toward the South China. Sea. The surrounding action offered the enemy three choices. Surrender, attempt to filter out through the lines at night, or use boats to get out of the small inlet, and into the South China. Sea.

Leaflets were dropped for days in the Crescent, offering safe conduct through the lines and surrender. The leaflets also warned that the use of boats, in an attempt to escape, would not be tolerated, The U.S. Forces had put their white hats on again by offering options, The leaflets gave the enemy a cut off date for a departure by boat. After that time they would be blown out of the water. 'All aboard, all ashore that's going ashore!'.

Captain Baker could hardly wait for the cut off date. It was a chance for some sea action. The moment of truth was fast approaching for the enemy forces. Any boats beyond a 100 meter limit from the shore were fair game, and in a 'free fire zone'. Baker began singing 'anchors away', for the first time in years!

For some strange reason, the Troop Corn financier asked for volunteers for the mission, It wouldn't have been necessary, the gunship pilots were chomping at the bit. And Baker, above all, was the first man with his hand up when the role was called. Baker was selected to lead the heavy gunship team into the inlet at first light the following morning.

The three helicopter heavy team took off just as the sun began to offer the first sign of light over the horizon. The gun crews had eaten a. quick breakfast and excitement was in the air!

The flight to the crescent area was low level, as always. But because of the enemy activity in the Bong Son plains and the Crescent area, the gunships stayed lower than normal.

The three gunships snaked their way north through any opening available. Below tree top level when possible, taking advantage of low lying hills and wooded areas for protection. In the wide open area, they skimmed the ground, alternating the direction of flight to one side or the other, to avoid providing a. target for an enemy gun crew. During the flight they were always working their way east towards the inlet.

The ground became sandy, and the dunes began to rise just before the inlet from the South China Sea. The gunships continued to work their way between the dunes as they approached the target area. The hilly dunes offered protection from detection. Baker was so positive of what would be found in the inlet, he radioed the other gunships and told them to arm the rocket pods.

The four NVA soldiers in the largest boat had just pulled away from the small fishing village on the inlet shore, Their narrow skiff was headed out towards the open sea. Each soldier had a paddle and was in fine rowing form, each stroke in unison as if they were coxswain controlled.

The four Vietnamese could hear the loud popping of the helicopter blades as they produced the small sonic boom at the tips. It didn't concern them at the time because they had been hearing the same type of noise for days as they were being pushed out towards the sea. Half of the time, they never saw the source of the noise.

Baker added a some forward cyclic at the last dune and a little bit of collective pitch to ease ahead of the other two helicopters and at the same time gain some altitude at the last possible moment.

Baker knew that a flat trajectory with the rockets wouldn't be as good against a. boat as a steeper angle. The target would offer a very low target, with very little exposed above the water line, Baker's Navy experience was paying off again!

Baker popped up over the last dune to reveal what he had predicted. The small boat with the four occupants looked like the Yale racing team.

Because of the slight upward pressure of the collective, the first pair of rockets fired were long. Baker adjusted the sight slightly. The next pair were dead center into the side of the boat and midway between the four NVA oarsmen.

The remaining two gunships selected targets in the inlet and were busily doing their thing to stop the exodus to the South China Sea.

Baker was hovering over the floating debris from the first boat that he had sunk. One of the occupants survived and was coming up for air, getting a mouthful and then sinking below the surface again.

Each time the NVA surfaced, he would expose only what was necessary to get air. The water was deep, there was no way that Baker and his crew was going to attempt an extraction from the water without knowing what the NVA held in his hands. The NVA was well known for the suicidal tendencies and Baker didn't want to be a team member for the grenade throw.

Baker could see the man below the surface of the water, He instructed the door gunner to get ready to fire when the man surfaced. Because of the angle, the door gunner could not see the man in time. He managed to fire in the wrong place each time the NVA surfaced

Finally, Baker removed his .30 caliber carbine from the back of his armor seat and made certain the selector was on full automatic, The next breath of air for the NVA was also filled with carbine rounds

The remaining boats in the inlet were small. Each capable of holding one passenger each, The NVA were hidden under the tarps or under the gunnels of the small boats.

Baker hovered over to one of the boats and held the aircraft over it as the door gunner dropped a fragmentation grenade into it. As soon as the grenade was released, the helicopter slid off to the side and waited for the results. Baker then radioed the other two aircraft and told them to save the rockets and to use grenades to finish the .i ob.

vi

Baker was getting proficient at bunker building. The closer he was to rotation time, the more sandbags he filled. The area around LZ English had hard ground. But, by using the issue entrenching tool, Baker was able to fill the bags rapidly.

His sleeping area was in the corner of one of the big General Purpose tents. He had purposely selected the corner so that he could easily roll into the bunker in the event of a night attack by the enemy.

Baker's rocket box pallet for his air mattress was in the corner. It kept him off of the damp ground. Around the pallet, he constructed a narrow shelf which contained the necessities of life. One .38 caliber revolver (which he had decided, a long time ago, was only good for one purpose, In the event capture was imminent), one single barrel 40mm grenade launcher with a small bandolier of shells, his trusty MS carbine with a metal container of 500 rounds and finally, a half a dozen fragmentation grenades.

In the event of attack, Baker would be able to roll out of his bed and into the adjoining bunker. The bunker had small firing apertures and the armament that he had amassed, was within easy reach.

V

A cease fire between the opposing forces had been declared for TET, the Vietnamese celebration of the Lunar New Year. The white hat syndrome again. No one called a cease fire for the New Year recognized by the U.S. Forces.

Cease fires were different in southeast Asia than in the other wars experienced by Americans in the past. In "All's quiet on the Western front", there was a 'no mans land'. In South Viet Nam, every place was no mans land!

TET offered a chance to rest. And, it also offered more opportunity for Baker to continue with the construction of his bunker. He had almost accomplished a three bag thick wall which would stop most rounds.

And, at night, there was the opportunity to write home or visit Billy Garner to exchange goody box contents.

Billy Garner had just received a package from home and had invited Bob Baker over to his tent to have some of the cheese, smoked sausage and if they were lucky, some fresh crackers.

Bob Baker got his aluminum bowl out and heated bath water on the gasoline stove. The Air Force showers were no longer available, so a sponge bath would have to do. Stepping into some fresh, river washed, fatigue pants Baker was ready to go. He opened the tent flap into a moon lit night to make the 100 foot trip to Billy's tent.

"Bang, ziiiing!" The sniper couldn't resist the target. Here was some idiot walking out into the moonlit night wearing a white T shirt. Baker dove for cover and low crawled back into his tent. Damn! There goes the evening meal. Baker yelled his regrets to Billy's tent. Billy fell out of his 'Z machine' laughing.

VI

During the TET cease fire, the troop continued recon missions throughout the LZ English area, just to keep everyone honest. Baker was on one of the missions, early in the morning, when he located a number of flag poles, with NVA flags.

Apparently, there had been a very important political meeting overnight and the enemy had raised flags. The poles were bamboo, refusing to remain upright when the helicopter hovered near them. Each time the crew got close enough to grab one of the flags, the bamboo would flex away from the aircraft. Finally, after a lot of effort, Baker and his crew retrieved all of the flags.

Night missions were also required along Highway One to make certain that the enemy wasn't moving fresh replacements or materials during TET. The troop gunships were used in a blacked out condition to patrol the road all night long, reporting any activity.

Baker pulled the assignment for the first night and was alternating the mission with other gunships from the troop to keep a constant watch on the highway.

Baker had just lifted off of the pad and was north of LZ English when he received automatic weapons fire from a position along the highway. From the air, at night, the tracer rounds were so heavy, it looked like a red hose.

Baker radioed the information in to the troop operations and requested permission to return fire, "Red 22, this is Red Charger 3, request is denied, that is a friendly position!" "Roger, Red Charger 3, I'm sure as hell glad that they aren't mad at me!".

This was not an isolated case of 'friendly fire'. The Troop had experienced it before. One of the scout pilots had flown low level over a hill north of LZ English a week before and had suddenly come upon a South Vietnamese infantry unit patrolling alongside highway one. Whether startled, or maybe politically inclined to the left, no one would ever know, One of the infantry men simply opened up on the U.S. made helicopter with his U.S. made weapon.

Once one man had started the firing at the helicopter, the entire unit opened up and the U.S. made weapons shot down the U.S. made helicopter, drilling a neat hole through the pilots U.S. made leg. The pilots of the Troop didn't consider this to be cricket.

Lt. Wentsworth experienced a similar incident with different results while flying between Bong Son and An Khe.

The highway between the Bong Son plains and the valley where the First Cavalry Division resided was secure. It contained an unending line of trucks and vehicles with supplies from the rear area, to the troops in the jungle.

The security of the highway, and the bridge that spanned a small river, was the responsibility of the South Korean forces. They were tough and they did a good job. Boredom, or one of those irresistible urges will cause people to do strange things.

During one trip from An Khe, Lt. Wentsworth was low level on the road to Bong Son. He approached the small bridge that had one S, Korean soldier at each end of it.

As he approached the bridge, he saw the S. Korean raise his rifle and fire a. round at him. The other S. Korean followed suit as Wentsworth passed over the east end of the bridge. When Wentsworth arrived at the laager area he reported the incident to the operations officer.

Within a few days word came back from the S. Korean command. They were very apologetic and offered guidance. "If it happens again, return fire!".

The following day, it happened again to Lt. Wentsworth. Following the guidance, he calmly blew both S. Koreans off each end of the bridge.

CHAPTER SIX

MAJOR NATHAN DREDD was becoming known for his skill at the controls of the Command and Control ship. He didn't have any.

Whenever Dredd managed to get his head out of his hands and his butt out of the chair in the operations tent, he managed to get in the way.

He damaged one aircraft by hitting a raised area during an approach to a landing pad, and on numerous occasions, during operations, he had been told to get out of the way by one or more of the gunship pilots.

Dredd was simply not good Troop Commander material. He was likeable, and he portrayed interest, but it was obvious to everyone that he was self serving. Dredd was a mill stone around the necks of everyone.

During an operation, shortly after Dredd's arrival as Troop Commander, a gunship had gone down in a valley near Bong Son. The crew was safe, but an extraction was required immediately. In the past, getting the crew out had been the first priority.

By the time Dredd made the decision to get the infantry and gunships in the air, the enemy had managed to move in close and were lobbing mortar rounds at the downed aircraft. For the first time since Baker's arrival, a crew came close to being lost due to slow reaction time.

When the lift ship made the crew extraction, the enemy was dangerously close to making a capture. The lift ship was receiving fire as they pulled the crew out. Had the Troop commander made the decision to cover the crew sooner, the threat of losing a crew would not have existed.

During the latter part of the extraction, Dredd arrived on the scene in the command and control helicopter. The gunships were suppressing the enemy fire, and the situation was well in hand. Nothing remained but the downed aircraft, which was not salvable

A few weeks later, it was discovered that Dredd had been put in for a Distinguished Flying Cross for his part in the operation. The other pilots had not been mentioned in the citation.

Captain Baker avoided Dredd like the proverbial plague. He had already been in one or two small encounters with the Major and wanted to avoid any further contact if possible.

ii

"Captain Baker, Major Dredd wants to see you in the operations tent!". "Crap, what did I do now", Baker thought to himself. "I'm getting too short for any long conversations with that dumb son of a bitch' ".

"Captain Baker, I've never fired the 40mm grenade launcher and have been told that you are the one to teach me!". Dredd continued, "I'll fly with you tonight, and after the mission, we'll fire the launcher out in the free fire zone!"

The night mission went smoothly. No enemy fire was received during the flight along highway i, and, so far the time with Dredd had not been too bad. He was likeable, and he talked a good game, So far, so good. Baker was beginning to think that all that he had felt and heard about Dredd was wrong.

After the firing demonstration of the 40mm 'chunker' and Dredd's indoctrination with the gun, the aircraft was headed towards the troop laager area, for refuel and rearming. Dredd was in the left seat of the helicopter and wanted to make the approach to the pad.

As the aircraft turned towards the final leg of the landing, Captain Baker said, "watch this helicopter Major, it is very nose heavy because of the added rounds of ammunition in the back!". Dredd answered in the affirmative on the intercom and started the landing.

Baker had just started to remove his hand from the cyclic control after using the intercom button when he noticed the circular motions in the stick. Baker hesitated and then lightly placed his hand back on the stick. The closer the helicopter got to the ground, the bigger the circular motions became until they had reached a six inch circular pattern, Finally, Baker added pressure to stop the motion of the cyclic and held the aircraft on a steady approach path until it touched down.

Once on the ground, Major Dredd asked, "did you take control of the aircraft on short final?" Baker assured Major Dredd that he had, in fact, over ridden the Major on the controls. "Why?", was the question, "Because I don't want to die!", was the answer. Dredd and Baker stayed as far apart as possible after the incident.

Helicopters are a critical piece of machinery, under the best of conditions, Overloaded, they are super critical. The rotor plane of a helicopter is like the wing of a fixed wing aircraft, lift is derived from the wing, and erratic movements of the rotor plane destroy lift, Baker's overloaded aircraft required very smooth and delicate handling, a loss of lift during approach tended to cause the aircraft nose to tuck under.

iii

The U.S. infantry unit was under heavy enemy fire, and the source could not be located. The U.S. troops knew it was coming from the general area of the river that ran north and south. B troop had been requested to assist in finding and destroying the source.

The infantry Captain got in the back of the UH1B gunship at L.Z English, "Captain, rny unit is under fire, and I would like to check that river bank for the NVA!", Baker acknowledged the Captain and pulled pitch for the river, and the friendly unit.

Baker, along with WO2 Richley, had been working on the helicopter to provide a better chance of survival in the event they were downed. Extra water had been stored in the back along with C rations, In addition, they made certain there was plenty of ammunition for the weapons they would need in the event they had to E&E (escape and evade) an area.

One item that was added was a star cluster shell which could be fired from a M79 grenade launcher. The grenade launcher had been added to the back of the seat, along with rounds, and the star cluster shell. The pyrotechnic shell would be handy as a method of signaling the location of the crew if they were down in an area of heavy undergrowth.

It was like Deja Vu. Baker had just rounded the curve in the river and there were three NVA soldiers staring up at him from the water. They were up against the bank adjoining the wooded area, and neck deep in the water.

Baker started a turn to the left and noticed that one of the enemy soldiers was starting across stream to the sparsely wooded area on the other side. Baker's favorite type of target!

Just above the trees, and at the usual hover, Baker told Richley to hold the aircraft in position while he got the sighting device down, trained it on the NVA, on the other side of the river, and began pumping 40mm rounds at the fleeing target

Fifteen rounds into the mission, and all hell broke loose in the gunship. The remaining two NVA, still in the water, opened up at the gunship directly overhead. Rounds from the AK47's entered the aircraft on the left side, one round went through the fleshy part of the infantry Captain's leg. The left side of the aircraft next to Baker was riddled

The inside of the gunship cockpit suddenly filled with smoke and small white hot stars as the star cluster shell exploded after being hit, The smoke was thick enough to cut. So thick, the instrument panel was no longer visible. The little white stars danced and ricocheted lazily around the inside of the cockpit, and it wasn't even the 4th of July!

Baker suddenly realized that they were still at a hover. The last time he saw outside, they were right on top of the trees. Mow, he or Richley couldn't see anything inside or outside. Baker took the controls and gently added a. little forward cyclic collective pitch.

He then slammed the window of the cockpit open. The smoke was removed immediately to reveal that they were climbing out, and away from the trees.

Several of the rounds had entered the left door, waist high for Baker, ricocheting off of the armor plate on the seat behind him, slamming into the instrument panel. The damage to the instruments was extensive. The critical gauges for engine temperatures, RPM's and altitude were gone.

Baker and his crew returned the Captain to the medical tent, While enroute, Richley noticed blood on the back of Baker's fatigues, Baker had been wounded. Baker thought to himself, "I must be losing my touch, the rounds came in my side of the aircraft'"

At the medical tent, Baker was told that he would have to be hospitalized to make certain that the round had not entered a critical area in the chest cavity.

The hospital stay in Qui Nhon was pleasant. After his arrival, Baker was told the wounds were not serious but that he looked like he could use some rest. The doctor prescibed five days in bed. It had sounded great, but after three days. Baker couldn't stand the quiet anymore and left the hospital to return to the unit.

iv

The gunships in the troop always carried the extras which might be needed for any occasion. There was the extra. C rations and water, personal weapons, compasses and other items needed in the event the crew found themselves on the ground without a personal invitation. Each helicopter carried a liberal supply of grenades strung across a wire behind the door gunner and crew chief. The collection would consist of CS (persistent tear gas), several colors of smoke, fragmentation grenades and WP(white phosphorous).

Lt. Wentsworth's new gunner had just replenished the supply of smoke, grenades and WP in his helicopter. During the process, he had attached one of the WP grenades to the wire with the grenade pull ring. This might not have caused any problem if the cotter pin holding the ignition spoon down hadn't been squeezed together, instead of flared out as normal.

The gunship was on a mission covering infantry on the ground, they had landed several times and with each bump, the cotter pin worked it's way slowly out of the hole. On the final mission for the day, the pin was finally freed.

The White Phosphorous grenade dropped onto the seat, between the door gunner and crew chief, where it exploded, Both crew chief and gunner were severely burned. The pilot and co-pilot were badly burned on the back of their necks and shoulders from the hot sticky material.

V

The small detachment of three men from the 30th Engineer Regiment, NVA, worked slowly down the bank of the river in the darkness. It was after 2 A.M. in the morning, there was a quarter moon.

The moonlight was not enough to reveal the three explosive experts. They had taken great care in rubbing the mud on their bodies to remove any chance of reflection from the moon. Although the lower part was washed away, the exposed upper torso was sufficiently covered.

As they approached the bridge, each man shifted the heavy load of plastic explosives that he carried. They had practiced this operation over and over, and had no intention of being under the bridge for longer than fifteen minutes, The three would split up, set the charges, the trip wires and be gone, All within the time limit.

The Navy river patrol boats had been patrolling the area to the north for the past six weeks, making trips under the bridge several times each day. The NVA colonel in command of the operations in the Bong Son area had decided to put a stop to the patrol boat action.

The charges were placed on each side of the center pilings, and at each end of the bridge. They were Placed in such a manner that the explosion would not destroy the bridge, but would destroy anything moving under the bridge, The NVA had future plans for the bridge and wanted it intact.

vi

Captain Baker and WO2 Richley were north of LZ English, They had just turned south to head back for refueling, when Richley noticed a lone IWA running through the woods below them, He turned towards the man and pointed him out to Baker.

Baker got the mechanism down for the 40mm turret and moved the sights onto the running NVA just as Richley started a shallow dive, "Chunk, chunk, chunk", "CRACK!"

They had been sucked in again. The running NVA was the running rabbit at the dog track, The crack was from a direct hit in the center of the windshield. Baker's windshield! Somewhere along the tree line, a sharpshooter with a SKS rifle had Plowed one into the aircraft windshield.

WO2 Richley looked at Baker, looked at the hole in the windshield, and looked at Baker again, It was an impossibility, but it happened. The round hit dead center in the windshield, had passed through the sighting device for the 40mm, bypassed Baker's thick head and disappeared out the back door of the gunship without touching anything. Baker had his helmet faceshield down and he hadn't even been cut by the Plexiglas.

The gunship continued the 40 mm run while Baker continued to fire, Finally, the rabbit could no longer run.

Richley thought it was amazing. Baker thought (to himself) "my luck is changing, they've finally found my side of the aircraft!", That night, Baker put another row of sandbags on the top of his bunker and looked at the calendar. He was down to less than 20 days, and he had a bad case of the 'double digit fidgets'. He was beginning to fear that he wouldn't make it. v

It was nearly a year since Baker's arrival in South Viet Nam. It had been a tough transition from the pleasantries of every day life in the real 'world', to the stark reality of South Viet Nam.

During the year, Baker had made a complete turn around. When he first arrived in country and was assigned to B Troop, 1/9th, he readily accepted death as a. strong possibility.

Because of his acceptance, he took chances. He hadn't really tried to avoid the gunfire. In many cases he flaunted it. But, he wasn't different than the other members of the troop.

Each new member of the troop, at least those in the helicopters, seemed to go through a period of acceptance, then invulnerability, and eventually, awareness. A conscious awareness that he had reached the end of the tour, and just might make it after all!

Baker had reached the awareness point of his tour. Orders from the pentagon had been received, detailing him to Fort Wolters Texas as a flight instructor in helicopters. Letters from home were all directed towards the return to civilization. Letters from friends were beginning to slow to a. trickle, with "it won't be long now, we'll talk about it when you get back" statements.

The wrinkled, wet, musty and dirty class A uniform was pulled out of the duffle bag and sent to the local laundry. The 'laundry', consisted of two Vietnamese women beating the uniform on some rocks in the river, while a company of NVA were pissing in it upstream. But no one would notice, unless they stood too close to you.

Actually. Baker was beginning to get scared. There were too many last minute changes for Bob to allow himself to get cocky about going home. He had heard too many stories about the last day, and the last mission, and the bullet with your name on it.

Bob's replacement was in the unit and had been briefed, trained and had completed the in country orientation, His first command decision was to pull everyone off combat missions when they reached 30 days prior to rotation.

This had delighted everyone. Bob was no exception. He spent the extra, time getting his bunker reinforced, and began to relax. He'd taken his share of fire, and on top of it, the rounds were starting to hit his side of the aircraft. So, it was time to lay off.

One illness and one emergency leave settled that. Within 3 days after the initiation of the '30 day-rule', Bob was back in the gunships flying combat missions. It was less than ten days until Bob's big silver bird flew off, into the sunset, and the world.

All of the gunship pilots had been assembled for special training. They were going to receive instruction with flame throwers. "Flame Throwers?" everyone had screamed, You've got to be joking!

No one was joking. Each pilot received individual instruction on the use of the back pack flame thrower. Some one had come up with the unique idea that the flame throwers could be used, at a hover, from the gunships. Apparently, the officers and warrant officers were going to be the operators of the new addition to the gunship armament. It was definitely time for Baker to go home.

vi

With only five days to go, Baker returned to the rear area at An Khe for out processing, and the flight home. It was the first time that he had seen his forty dollar real estate investment in six months.

Prior to departing the Troop laager area, the officers and warrant officers were ushered in to see the Squadron Commander. It was his chance to say thank you, and goodbye.

WO2 Jacobson had arrived in country with Baker, and was departing on the same plane back to the States. The colonel said goodbye to Baker and then proceeded to berate Jacobson for the accident at the refueling point six months earlier. Not once, during the conversation, did the Colonel say "thanks for a job well done!", In spite of the mishap, Jacobson had done a good job.

Billy Garner, because of his job as Maintenance Officer, had good reasons to be back at An Khe. And, he made it a point to be there during the time Bob was getting ready to go home. Going home was great, but it was tough on those who still had time to wait before it was their turn.

Billy and Bob Baker sat in Garner's hooch that first night discussing all of the events of the past year. They were drinking beer and relaxing for the first time in months.

Garner's hooch was hand built of ammunition boxes. The only materials purchased had been some two by four studs. The outside was completely covered with the knotty pine material from the rocket boxes.

Billy had gone several steps further. He, and his hooch mate had built dressers from the same pine material. The dressers even had drawers.

The two were sipping their third beer for the evening when they both heard a noise. The noise came from a rat, the size of a house cat. The rat was sitting in one of the open drawers of the dresser. It sat there, peering at Bob and Billy.

Billy signaled Baker to be quiet. He slowly raised his arm up over his head and removed the .45 caliber automatic that was hanging from the shoulder holster over his bed.

Billy steadied the big colt .45 on his knee, cocked the hammer, and promptly blew a hole through the dresser front, and his hooch mates class A uniform. The rat smiled and wandered off.

vii

Lt. Wentsworth, and his crew, just completed the mission covering the infantry company, The mission was a. piece of cake. They had chalked up nine KIA's. The crew was exuberant about the day, The mission had run smoothly, and the infantry commander had been Pleased with their efforts.

The crew was just north of LZ English and were returning to the laager area, for refuel and rearmament. It was late, and they were finished for the day.

Carl Wentsworth stared at the bridge, off to the right of the helicopter, as they headed south, Suddenly, he said, "I've got the aircraft!". His co-pilot released his hands from the controls as Wentsworth took over.

Wentsworth started a shallow dive and a. slight right turn to get the aircraft lined up with the bridge. The warrant officer asked, "where are we going, lieutenant?", Wentsworth replied, "under the bridge!"

The UH1B gunship leveled off from the dive. It was just above the water as it headed for the bridge. There was no doubt about it, the water in the river was down, and there was plenty of clearance.

The co-pilot and the two door gunners were enjoying the fast and low flight as they approached the bridge. Their smiles suddenly turned to horror as they caught a last minute glimpse of the black wire stretched the width of the river, Just then, the skids of the aircraft made contact.

The explosion could be heard for several miles around the bridge. The fireball, and the black smoke, from the remaining JP4 fuel rose to three thousand feet. Along with what remained of the crew.

viii

Baker had eaten the evening meal, had a few beers with Billy Garner and was re-packing his small suitcase for the third time. Each time, more items had been eliminated. Baker was down to one handbag instead of the two he had started with.

He took two of the small white pills. The doctor said only one was necessary, but he had to get some sleep. Baker was wound up like a piece of tightly coiled spring steel, and the last two nights had been fitful.

The combination of the two valiums and the three beers must have done it. Baker finally came to the next morning at 10 o'clock.

During the night, the VC had probed the perimeter, just behind Baker's hooch. The enemy had been fired upon by the Aerial Rocket Artillery unit, and, in return, had popped a dozen mortar rounds into the camp. The alert had lasted for nearly two hours, while Baker slept.

The flight to Pleiku was short. The returnees would spend the night in a barracks where they could get a hot shower and avail themselves to an overnight laundry facility.

The next day, the big jet aircraft from Pan American Airways landed at the Pleiku airfield. It wasn't on the ground long before the passengers were loaded. Shortly after takeoff, and the aircraft leveled off, the stewardesses served the first meal. Steak and eggs. Baker knew then, he was back in the real world.

CHAPTER SEVEN

IN 1957, FORT Wolters Texas was a. hub of activity. Located on highway 180, 35 miles west of Fort Worth in Mineral Wells, it was the primary helicopter training center for the U.S. Army.

Captain Robert Baker arrived at Fort Wolters in June. After establishing his family in quarters on post, Baker started the MOI (Methods of Instruction) to become a. flight instructor in the helicopter.

The training at Fort Wolters was divided into two phases of training. Pre-solo primary and primary. Baker was to be assigned to the pre-solo primary phase, which meant the students arriving at his aircraft each day, had no prior flying experience. "Gentlemen, this is a helicopter!"

After pre-solo flight training for eight weeks, the student graduated to the primary phase. The eight weeks of primary was directed towards cross country, night flying, confined areas and other advanced maneuvers.

Fort Wolters was like a beehive during flight training periods each day. During any one four hour block of training, either in the morning or afternoon, 750 or more helicopters were in the sky over Mineral Wells. And, that was only half of the fleet.

Baker would be instructing in the TH55 helicopter. The TH stood for Training Helicopter. Designated a Hughes 269A in civilian aviation, it is a two passenger, side by side helicopter. The main rotor system was driven by eight 'V Belts' from the engine to the transmission case.

The helicopter was small, but it had ample power and was comfortable to fly over long periods of time. Unless you were a. student.

Unlike the Bell 'Hueys', the throttle control did not have a. governor. It required constant work for the student pilot to maintain the needles in the green, and married (together). With each change in collective pitch control, a throttle correction was necessary. And with each collective and throttle change, a change in anti-torque pedal was necessary.

The pitch control changed the angle of the rotor blades. The bigger the bite, the more lift. Up to a point, that was true. Rotor blades being much like wings, they were subject to stall also. But, with an increase of the pitch came a. slow down in engine RPM's and anti-torque RPM'S. The throttle increases or decreases were in direct correlation with rotor pitch.

Learning to fly a TH55 was like learning to walk a tightrope across the Niagara. Falls while carrying a washing machine, still running, and with the load off center.

The Hughes helicopter had a three bladed, fully articulated rotor system that would lead, lag, hunt, feather, pitch and yaw. Which meant, basically speaking, it was one hell of a mass of machinery, where anything could go wrong.

Prior to starting the helicopter, and during the pre-flight, each blade was inspected for damage and adjusted to a mark near the hub of the blade. A small arrow, would be placed on a mark near a hydraulic buffer, by moving the blade fore or aft.

This procedure centered each blade at exactly 120 degrees from the preceding blade. When the aircraft engine was started, and the rotor system clutch engaged, the rotors were in balance. Without the proper balance, the aircraft could literally shake itself to pieces.

After starting the engine and stabilizing the RPM's at 1250, the rotor engage switch was moved into the engage position, momentarily. As soon as a slight drop in RPM was detected, the switch was moved back to the center position, allowing the belts to catch up with the action of the engine and transmission.

The procedure was repeated, until the engine RPM and rotor needles 'married', or came together. By completing this in small steps, the blades slowly began to turn. This method prevented their being jerked out of the 120 degree spacing necessary for a balanced rotor system.

The pre-solo primary division was made up of a few military flights, with all military instructors. The rest were civilian contract instructors. The ratio in 1967 was 3 military and seven civilian flights.

Each flight consisted of a flight commander, assistant flight commander, operations officer and 20 to 25 instructors.

A flight received up to 80 students every ten weeks. The students went through eight weeks of intensive training. After the eight weeks, the instructors would go through two weeks of intensive drinking before the next new batch of students arrived.

Baker was assigned to one of the three military flights in 'C Division'. He was immediately made operations officer and assigned four new students.

Each student received a total of 80 hours of flight training in pre-solo primary before moving on to primary. The eighty hours were devoted to hovering, turns, traffic patterns, approaches and touch down autorotations.

After the initial orientation ride of one hour, the student began to receive the daily instruction for the course and, in turn, received a daily grade for his efforts. The first and hardest of all the training was learning how to hover the little beast.

ii

"Good morning gentlemen!" Major Baker yelled as he mounted the platform for the morning briefing of the class, "Good morning sir!", the class responded. Baker again yelled. "What color is Marine green?" "CHICKEN SHIT!" the class yelled.

Baker had his time as instructor in one of the flights and had learned a lot about students. During that time, he had also been the operations officer. After a few months in this capacity, Baker had been promoted. With the promotion came the chance to be a flight commander with his own instructors. Baker had readily accepted the opportunity, and, he loved it.

His present class of students was a mixed bag.

Ordinarily, the class would either consist of officers or Warrant Officer Candidates. This one was half and half, including six marine officers. Baker had prompted the class about the color of marine uniforms the first day and now would address the class the same way for eight weeks.

The class was in it's first week with Major Baker, his assistant flight commander Captain Bill Richarde and his operations officer

Captain Jimmy Simpson. They had been together for nearly a year now as a flight and had developed flight C-5 as the best in 'C Division'.

Hovering the TH55 was the first maneuver a student had to learn well, Texas winds are always strong. To hold the helicopter three foot off the ground and make pedal turns upwind, downwind, crosswind and stay over the spot in a Texas wind, required real skill. At this point in their training, the students felt lucky if they could hold it in a football stadium.

Baker stood out in front of the little portable control tower at the stage field and watched the dancing orange helicopters. Each of his 22 instructors had one student in a helicopter trying to teach the student to hover. The stage field that had been selected for the first week, was one of the largest. The students would need all of the room it provided for the hovering phase.

Even above the sound of the helicopters hovering in front of the tower, he could hear his assistant flight commander screaming at the student. "What the fuck are you looking at me for, dammit, look at the instruments and DO something!"

One helicopter zoomed up to 20 feet, at a hover, and Baker cringed. Get it down, get it down, he thought to himself. Down it came, lightly bounced off of the skids and then back to about 20 feet. Baker made a note to have the helicopter checked for hard landing.

Baker chuckled to himself, he remembered his flying time with C.Q. Stockwell in Alabama. When getting ready to land, 'Stock' would sometimes say, "always keep the greasy side down!". At least Baker's students were doing that.

One helicopter was over a spot, really nice!, at three feet, great!, except it was spinning to the right and the turns were getting tighter. Each class was a heart in the throat act at this point, and it didn't get better. The real thrills were yet to come. Solo week!

Students were always different, A flight instructor could never put his finger on two students, anywhere, and say they were identical. Each one had his own distinct problem, and each one had to be handled differently.

Some students required total coolness on the part of the instructor. If you screamed or yelled, they fell apart completely. If they received a low grade, they became unresponsive. Some, who deserved much lower daily grades progressed faster with the encouragement of a grade they didn't deserve.

Captain Richarde had drawn a student that required screaming. It was the only way to get the students attention, Bill was a fantastic officer. From Los Angeles, Bill had been associated with the Hell's Angels during his early years.

At some point in his life, Richarde had decided that wasn't the way to get ahead. He completed college and accepted a commission in the Army. Richarde was of average size, but built like a bull. He looked and sounded rough, scaring the hell out of most students at first. But Bill was a dichotomy. Richarde was a superb artist with oils.

Richarde, along with Simpson and the other 18 flight instructors were all veterans of at least one tour in South Viet Nam. The time at Fort Wolters was just an interim stopover on a guaranteed return trip to the jungles.

Every other week, an instructor would depart for his return trip to Southeast Asia, and another new instructor would arrive in the flight.

Baker gave each new instructor his own style of briefing. Each new instructor would be told that the student was at Fort Wolters for only one purpose, to try to kill his instructor.

Baker had learned that the hard way at Fort Rucker Alabama as a flight instructor in fixed wing aircraft. A student had inverted the L-19 'bird dog' at 300 feet altitude. Baker and student had plowed it into the 70' pine trees upside down and walked away, only by some miracle, In that case, Baker had not kept the 'greasy side down'.

By now, Baker had encountered most of the types of of student, but still had not seen any duplicates. As a flight commander, Baker was required to give 'prog' rides to students not showing progress.

Baker's final word determined whether they continued with additional time, were washed back to another class or were completely washed out of the program. A student that washed out returned to the Army ranks as a sergeant.

'Progress' rides were what the student feared most. Next came the flight check rides that were spaced within the 80 hours course at 40, 60 and 80 hours. The flight check rides were conducted by the Standardization Department check pilots.

Major Baker worked hard attempting to relax a. student that was required to take a 'prog' ride. He talked to them first, at length, to try to get them relaxed. During the flight he tried to encourage them with positive comments. Yet, with all of the laid back attempts, students completing a check ride or progress ride lost as much as three pounds through sweating.

Accurate details of the results of each check ride were maintained by the Department. Baker made it a point to visit the Standardization Department at the end of each class to see if there were common areas of weakness. If, so, the instructors from C-5 would work on that weakness during the next class. The end results were better and better final check ride grades with each class.

iii

Before moving on to the assignment as Flight Commander, Baker had been in one flight where he had been assigned to help the students that were having problems.

Baker's last student had been a Marine lieutenant who could not relax. The only thing that worked with him was fear. Whenever the marine had difficulties with a particular part of the curriculum Baker would threaten to write a letter to the Marine Commandant.

The student finally got it down pat. Baker had him pull over to the hardstand to land and got out of the aircraft. Baker said, "You can solo now, just do it right!" Baker went to the tower and watched the student make two good approaches to the pads.

The students third take off for the final and last approach was good. He climbed out to pattern altitude and then radioed "I've got an engine failure!" The tower operator talked him down as best he could as the aircraft disappeared behind the trees. Then a large cloud of dust appeared. The aircraft was totaled, but the student walked away.

iv

Auto rotations to the ground were a. required part of the curriculum. Each student was required to have a. minimum number of touch down autorotations during pre-solo primary. The purpose of the autorotation was to make emergency landings in the event of a power failure. Done properly, helicopters can be put on the ground safely with no damage.

An autorotation in the Hughes helicopter was like being on an elevator and having the cable snap. It was a quick ride down! When a pilot went into autorotation, he looked down between his feet that were on the anti-torque pedals, and that was where he was going to land, or crash.

By rolling the power off with the throttle, and immediately lowering the collective pitch, the blades are flattened out so that they will continue to rotate. The helicopter's attitude is maintained level until fifteen feet off the ground. At fifteen feet, aft cyclic control will slow the descent and forward movement at the same time.

With a little wind on the nose, a helicopter can be 'zeroed' out at this point (no forward movement). At 3 to 5 feet the aircraft attitude is again leveled and the remaining pitch available in the rotor blades is applied through the collective control. Baker could set a cup of coke on the console and make a touchdown autorotation without spilling a drop.

v

The mixed bag of students were still in their first week, learning to hover. WO2 Jose Martinez had a particularly difficult student. He was a 'leaner'. Students sat in the right seat of the helicopter (first pilot position in most helicopters). During the hovering training they would sometimes try to lean the helicopter into the position they wanted it.

Holding the helicopter over a spot is very difficult. By sitting straight up in the seat and applying the controls as necessary, the light will come on in about 8 to ten hours. But leaners were common. To correct the aircraft from drifting right, they would lean left. The more they leaned left, the more right cyclic they applied which caused the aircraft to drift further right. The student would eventually end up on the lap of the instructor, if the problem wasn't corrected.

At the end of the morning flight period. Jose Martinez went to Major Baker. "Sir, I have a problem with one of my students, he is a leaner". Jose continued, "I've tried everything with him, and nothing seems to work, so today, I did something that you may hear about". Baker waited with bated breath. Jose said, "The student kept leaning closer and closer", "I kept telling him to straighten up and it didn't work", "So finally, I kissed him on the cheek!"

The next morning when Major Baker addressed the class he talked about the leaning problem, He told the students there was an instructor in the class, who would remain unidentified, who could straighten out the leaning problem if it became necessary. Baker told them how the instructor responded to leaning. The class learned to hover in record time.

vi

Each training stage field consisted of six approach lanes with four pads on each lane. The field was divided into left and right traffic patterns. The two centermost lanes were generally used for straight in, touch down autorotations. The outer and second lane on each side was for practice approaches.

Based on this design, it was possible to have sixteen aircraft on final approach for landing at one time. It was an excellent design which made it possible to accomplish a lot of approaches in a four hour period of instruction.

After solo, each flight was assigned as many as 25 helicopters for a four hour block of instruction. Instructors and a student would fly to the stage field and the remaining helicopters would arrive flown by the students.

Each stage field had it's own tower and radio frequency, call sign, hot line to the medical evacuation helicopter at the main post, fire crew and mechanic. The same fire crew and mechanic were with the same flight on a permanent basis. If the flight moved to a different stage field, the same service personnel also moved.

Safety was a very important part of the training. The training center awarded desk sets with pen and pencils for 500 accident free hours of instruction in pre-solo primary. Not many were awarded. Because of the nature of the training, accidents were frequent, and many times fatal.

vii

The return to one of the three main post airfields at the end of a training day was particularly-hazardous. Seven hundred or more aircraft all converging into one area, at the same time, is mind boggling, Then consider the fact that a large number of the aircraft were being flown by-new students with 15 hours of flying experience.

At the end of a training period, it was common to see a 20 mile long entry leg for the main airfield. The end of the entry leg was sometimes at Weatherford Texas, within sight of Ft. Worth.

viii

Baker was operating the tower while the students were practicing the hovering at the stage field. One of the instructors had departed the stage field and was returning. Baker was watching, as the helicopter was entering the stage field pattern.

Off in the distance, the pattern for one of the main airfields was also visible. All of a sudden there was a. large fireball in the sky. Two of the helicopters had collided in mid air over Mineral Wells, Baker watched as the flaming debris of the wreckage and bodies fell from the sky to the parking lot of the Holiday Inn Motel.

Before Major Baker's tour was completed at Ft. Welters, he would see dozens of accidents and be selected to investigate one fatal accident involving poor maintenance.

CHAPTER EIGHT

DURING THE MIDDLE sixties, and the military buildup for Viet Nam, the Army flight program was in full swing, The airmobile army was becoming the latest concept, To be fully airmobile., there would be a big requirement for aviators.

While at Ft. Rucker as a Lieutenant, Baker witnessed the results of the buildup, The Army was advertising for aviators in some of the flying magazines.

The applicants, when accepted, arrived at Ft, Rucker as students. They were provided with the rank of WOW-1, and sent to primary flight school. The prerequisites to be considered, two hundred hours of flying time.

In the meantime, the Warrant Officer Candidate program was being expanded; and by 1967, be in full swing at Ft, Wolters Texas. C-5 flight would receive about 80 students every 10 weeks, There were 10 such flights in C Division.

Many of the candidates were volunteers direct from civilian life, Some of them came from the ranks of those who had enlisted prior to the program.

The candidates were dedicated, They worked hard, and were worked hard, They attended ground school for 4 hours a day and reported to the flight line for four hours. At the end of the school day, the tactical officers harassed them, providing the necessary regimentation. As a result, the number of dropouts was high.

The selection system for the WOC program was not easy. Only the best made it to the program, In spite of the selection process, there were a few culls that slipped through, and into flight school.

ii

Warrant Officer Candidate Sherman had been having some difficulties with ground school. The tactical officer ordered the WOC to report and explain why he was having problems.

Standing at attention, Sherman explained that he was on the Board of Directors for Federal Can Company, Because of his responsibilities as a board member, it was necessary for him to attend meetings in Dallas.

Sherman continued to explain that he had been drafted, Because of his interest in flying, Sherman entered the WOC flight program.

The tactical officer was thunderstruck. Here was someone attempting to make the best of a bad situation, The tactical officer was mature enough to realize that the curriculum at the flight school could cause a great deal of difficulties for a board member. He immediately made some arrangements for Sherman to be assigned to lighter du ties, with time available for the board meetings.

Because of the tactical officer's understanding, he and his wife were invited to go as guests of Sherman during the next weekend trip to the Bahamas, A leer jet and crew would fly Sherman, his wife, the tactical officer, his wife and some select friends to the islands.

The trip was fantastic for all. Money seemed to be no problem for Sherman. Sherman returned to his studies and his many new friends.

Occasionally, Sherman would ask a candidate or tactical officer for a loan, "because the stock broker had not mailed his dividend check yet", or, "because of a cash flow problem at Federal Can". In a. few weeks, the money was returned, Sherman got more popular each day.

One day there was a knock on the tactical officer's door, The man in the civilian clothes identified himself as a. member of the Army CID (Criminal Investigations Division),Apparently, there were some past due debts beginning to show up at the finance office, Flood would have been a better word.

Sherman turned out to be a first class fraud. He was not a board member of anything, let alone Federal Can Co, He would borrow money from one candidate or tactical officer to pay another, By repeating the process he always appeared to be paying his debts.

With each payment of a debt, Sherman's stature grew stronger in the financial world of Ft, Walters. The flight to the islands had beet-obtained through the same methods, with a payment now and then to cover the costs of the flight. No one had thought to actually contact Federal Can Company to verify Sherman's status.

iii

Lieutenant Colonel Robert Thacker commanded C Division, 'Blinky' was a quiet, soft spoken person. His wife Mimi, was not, The fact was, Mimi ran the division. When a new officer reported in to C Division, Mimi would check on his marital status.

Once Mimi found out that the officer was free, white and at least twenty, she would determine which flight he should be in, Bob and Mimi had a daughter, still single, and at home, She needed escorts for all of the functions.

Mimi was a party lady. Parties were frequent. Any excuse would do for a party. And, they were command functions, If Baker did not show up for a division party, the efficiency report would so reflect, As they always said in the army, "you'll read about it".

That was never a problem, Bob Baker liked Mimi. and Mimi liked Bob. Mimi heard all of the latest dirty jokes and Bob always returned the favor, with a new one for her, Mimi became the vibrant blood life of the division, She not only kept an eligible bachelor available to take her daughter to the parties, she kept the officer's and warrant officer's wives very busy.

When there was a function, the wives were totally involved in the organization of the affair. Each wife would be detailed to a specific task, and under the direct supervision of Mimi, As a result, most functions ran like clockwork.

A General's reception always presented a lot of pre-planning, Officer's and wives would arrive at a pre-designated time for introduction to the General, Officer's would be in dress blues with white shirt, bow ties and medals.

The wives, on the other hand, were required to wear a certain type of dress, along with a hat and gloves, or just a hat, or just gloves, The word on the apparel would be disseminated as soon as the General's wife made up her mind what she was going to wear.

iv

Week Two. The hovering was getting easier for the students, They had it pinned down to keeping the helicopter in a half acre square by now, and somewhere between the ground and fifteen feet.

Some students were way ahead of the others and caught on quickly with each new maneuver. The next week would be afternoons, with higher density altitude and stronger winds to contend with, The afternoon condition made it much tougher for the slow students.

Baker might consider opening up half of the stage field the next week for some of the advanced students. The instructors moving quickly to get them started on the normal approach and the traffic pattern, By the end of the week there was the consideration for student changes, Possibly one instructor with three students that did not have the hovering mastered.

Students having difficulties sometimes got the picture overnight, They located "the hover button", The hover button was like the left handed monkey wrench. It existed only in ones mind. But eventually, the students appeared to find the nonexistent hover button.

The instructor's were beginning to introduce autorotations into the training. The stage field mechanic would be busy each day determining if a 'hard landing' had occurred when one of the students over controlled the collective, Baker was getting more tense.

Another week of hovering, and the class should be well into the various approaches, Even the slow students would be ready by then.

V

Each graduating class of WOC students would leave Ft. Wolters with their mark on the post, The prank had become traditional. The jokes had ranged from changing the locks on the gates, to erecting signs indicating the post was closed.

The prank to end all pranks occurred in the latter part of 1968. It caused a lot of worry for everyone, especially the perpetrators.

The student had been assigned his aircraft number during his 'stick briefing'. The instructor told him to take aircraft number 18007, fly it to Hue stage field, practice normal and steep approaches for one hour and then wait for the instructor to get his daily dual instruction.

The primary-solo student went to the large parking area at Downing AAF and began looking for his aircraft. After searching for 15 minutes, he reported back to the maintenance shack to get a replacement.

The maintenance people made a note on the list of aircraft. 'Aircraft #18097 not on hardstand, check with maintenance'. That evening, the third trick maintenance personnel attempted to locate the helicopter.

Within a day or two, a complete search was under way. Still no sign of TH55, number 18007. The search continued for several weeks. The CID was notified, and all instructors were asked to look for the missing helicopter.

The fisherman had just cast his line off of the floating dock in the lake northeast of Mineral Wells. The line snagged on something. He pulled, jerked and worked until it was free, and continued casting. Then, he noticed the water had an oil slick, and began to investigate.

Finally, he caught a glimpse of something on the bottom of the lake. It was fairly large and it was orange.

The sheriff notified the Military Police who in turn notified the CID. The helicopter was on the bottom of the lake. There were no bodies or any indication of injuries. No one had been reported missing.

From the ensuing investigation, it was determined that someone removed the helicopter from the parking area, at night, and attempted to land it on the floating dock. During the attempt, the pilot landed too close to one edge of the dock, and the helicopter rolled over into the lake.

The graduating class remained at Ft, Wolters for another week, while the investigation continued. No one admitted to the prank, The investigation was eventually terminated.

vi

Week Three, The students finally had the basics of hovering, Enough to start on the approaches to the panels at the stage field, The pattern for the training would require Major Baker to spend more time in the tower and less in the sun.

Normal approaches to a panel are at 20 degrees of descent, After turning final at pattern altitude, the student uses a reference in the aircraft to learn what 20 degrees should look like, The reference can be a rivet, or mark, Once the 20 degrees is established, the collective is lowered and the rate of descent is slowed by aft cyclic.

The closing and descent speeds are regulated from that point on until the helicopter comes to a 3 foot hover over the panel. Ideally, this would be a steady, slowly descending and gradually slowing approach until the helicopter comes to a stop three foot over the panel.

To accomplish a normal approach, the pilot twists the power grip with his left hand to maintain RPM's. while raising and lowering collective. With his right hand, he controls the attitude of the helicopter by moving the cyclic stick back, forth, right and left, Not to be left out, his feet are constantly moving to change the pitch on the tail rotor blades, The tail rotor blades-maintain a lined up position with the runway. He will also be sweating a lot.

Takeoffs are either made from a hover, or from the ground. From a hover, the aircraft is turned right or left to clear, making certain that another aircraft is not in conflict with the takeoff. The RPM's are maintained constant with the left hand and collective is applied at the same time with a simultaneous forward movement of the cyclic to move the helicopter forward and into flight. Once the aircraft moves through 'translational lift', a normal climb is established.

Translational lift occurs when the helicopter is no longer hovering as a result of the compressed air, or bubble, beneath the aircraft. The helicopter is moved off the bubble and becomes airborne as it reaches translational lift, The helicopter shudders slightly when it moves into translational lift.

Each of Major Baker's instructors are carrying three students of their 'stick' (a stick includes the instructor and students assigned to him). The only exception the assistant flight commander and operations officer have two students because of their extra duties, Major Baker, as flight commander, did not carry students.

vi

Major Baker had received the orders the previous week. He was ordered to conduct a 'collateral investigation' into a fatal aircraft accident that had occurred the week before at Downing AAF. A collateral investigation is completed for civilian use, in the event of litigation. The official military investigation is not available to outside civilian interests.

The TH55, with instructor and student pilot had lifted off from one of the six take off pads at Downing AAF. It climbed out normally until it reached 390 feet. Then, the rotor system froze. The blades came to a complete stop. No possibility of autorotation.

Major Baker started at the rear of the hangar where the wreckage was placed for the military investigation, He was not permitted to use their findings, and the military board could not use his. Baker started his investigation by taking pictures of the wreckage, After the straight downward fall from 300 feet, little remained; other than a 18" pile of aluminum.

Baker began reading up more thoroughly on the construction of the Hughes TH55. He found that the main mast which drove the rotor system from the transmission area was suspended in the housing by a 'thrust bearing'. With a little more effort, he found that the thrust bearing had frozen.

Further checking revealed that Hughes Corp. had recommended the change of the thrust bearing at 250 hours. The bearing was to be applied to the main mast by the 'heat differential' method.

According to the instructions, the mast was to be placed in a large freezer to contract, while the bearing was warmed and expanded in an oven, The procedure made the bearing installation less difficult.

Major Baker checked with the civilian contract maintenance supervisor. The bearings were being changed every 500 hours instead of 250, With further questions, Baker found that the freezer for the masts was being used to keep lunches cold, and the oven for the bearings was being used to heat the lunches.

When questioned about the method of applying the new bearings, Baker was told they were using an oversize pipe (larger than the diameter of the mast) to drive the bearings onto the mast. By doing so, the application of force onto the inner race of the thrust bearing was damaging the bearings between that point and the outer race.

From that day on, when Baker picked up a TH55 helicopter to fly, he would push the rotor system through several times until he had free wheeling speed on the blades, then reach up to the housing to feel for any vibrations. He repeated the free wheeling procedure a second time so he could place his ear on the housing to listen for any grinding noises. Even with the precautions, Baker broke out in a cold sweat each time he climbed out of the traffic pattern in the helicopter.

vii

Week Four, "What color is Marine green?" "CHICKEN SHIT!", the class responded. It was the beginning of the solo flights. The class ready, with a few exceptions, and class spirit very evident.

During the past weekend, Major Baker and his wife had two parties to attend, He had a hangover that would last all day long, It turned out to be a fun weekend, in spite of the head.

One of the parties had been a hail and farewell for C Division. Blinky made a few speeches to those departing and welcomed those arriving, Mimi nodded approval and sized up the incoming officers for rings. Those without rings received a stamp of approval, like a side of beef, Baker's wife asked Mimi for the third time during the week if there was any word on the upcoming General's reception: 'Hat, gloves, neither or both?'

WO2 Jergensen was an instructor in Major Baker's flight, Pete being single, brought a good looking platinum blonde to the party. Baker had a hard time keeping his eyes off her. Baker had a stamp that he wanted to use too!

Finally, Jergensen approached Major Baker and said. "Not bad, is she?" Baker nodded his approval. Jergensen said, "100 dollars, and you can have her for the night!"

Baker's mouth dropped open, He just started to speak when Jergensen explained. Pete had a stable of prostitutes, His stock in trade came out of the girls college in Denton Texas. Baker had always wondered about Pete's lavender Cadillac.

viii

The normal and steep approaches were looking good. Baker was just thinking to himself, "The normal approaches were the only weak areas, according to standardization, maybe this class will look even better".

"Tuy Hoa tower, this is army 18350, I have a first solo". "Roger 18350, instruct him to stay in the left hand traffic", Major Baker then made the blanket call, "Tuy Hoa traffic, this is the tower, we have a first solo, please clear the left hand pattern ! i!.

Pete Jergensen got out of the helicopter in front of the tower, buckled his shoulder harness to the seat belt on his side so that it would be secure, and paused to give the student a few last minute instructions.

Major Baker could see the students eyes from the tower, They looked like the pizza that he had eaten the night before. At least, they were as large, Baker had seen it before, time and time again, The apprehension for the first solo flight, It scares the hell out of them, he thought to himself. But once they make the first three trips around the pattern by themselves, the confidence is there, never to be lost!

Pete finished the last minute briefing and turned towards the tower, took his helmet off, and grinned at Major Baker, Nothing like pride in your work. Wonder if Pete grins when he puts the girls out on the corners?

WO2 Jergensen had walked about fifteen paces towards the tower, when the student lifted the helicopter up to a 3 foot hover, panicked and slammed it back on the ground, lifted it again, slammed it back again and then went to about fifteen feet with the engine screaming a pitch that was definitely over red line, The last slam to the ground curled the skids up to the doors on both sides.

With each bang, followed by the high pitched engine scream, Jergensen's steps faltered and his head hung lower. It appeared to Major Baker that he was about to cry.

"Tuy Hoa tower, this is Army 18350, 'stuttering', I think I might have an engine over speed!", "Roger 18350, shut it down!", Engine over speeds in any kind of aircraft require a complete tear down of the engine before the aircraft can be flown again.

CHAPTER NINE

THE PAST FEW weeks had gone well for WOC class 69-13, all of the students had soloed in the TH55. Most were getting proficient with the approaches, the traffic pattern, and the autorotations. Now, it was just a matter of polishing them up, in preparation for the final check rides.

WOC Borden was sweating like a hog going to slaughter. He had been notified the day before that he would be going for a progress ride with the flight commander the next day. He hadn't slept because of the worry.

Major Baker had been briefed on Borden's progress. He was only having one minor problem, and the flight instructor couldn't get it solved. All of Borden's approaches looked like a stairway, from the side. Instead of a smooth steady descent and approach to the panel, it was down, then forward, then down, all the way to the panel.

Major Baker had talked to WOC Borden prior to going to the hardstand for the helicopter. As usual, Bob tried very hard to instill confidence in the student. He bought the student coffee and then tried to explain how important it was to be relaxed during the 'prog ride'. As flight commander, he always wished that a magic powder was available to sprinkle on students to get them cooled off and less nervous.

The flight commander and the student located their helicopter and Bob watched as the student pre-flighted the machine. Bob paid particular attention to the rotor system and 'free wheeled' it through a few times to feel and listen to the area where the thrust bearing was located.

After strapping in, Bob watched as the student completed the pre-start procedures and then the start. Radio checks were completed, and the student picked the aircraft up to a hover. Bob noticed immediately that his 3 foot hover was erratic, and made a note of it. As soon as the Major jotted the note down, the student noticed and started sweating profusely.

Hovering turns for clearance were completed, and the student lowered the nose slightly then added collective and power to make the takeoff. As the aircraft climbed out, Major Baker turned around in his seat to look up at the rotor system, then remembered his first hour in a helicopter in the 'qualification course' at Ft. Rucker, Alabama.

In 1965, Baker had been a student in the 'Q course' at Ft. Rucker. The instructor had shown him a few things in the OH13 and then had said, "relax and light a cigarette, if you want". Baker had lit up, and was looking around.

When Baker turned to look up at the rotor system, the instructor had yelled, "DON'T DO THAT!" Baker had said, "What?". The instructor had said, "Don't ever look at the rotor system while you are flying, it will scare the shit out of you!!" They had both laughed, and agreed that there was an enormous number of moving parts in one place that could go wrong at any time.

Baker loved flying helicopters, so he turned back in his seat and quit looking at the bearing housing, the linkages, the blade grips, the turn buckles, safety wire. Jesus nut and everything else that was crucial to keeping the mass of spinning machinery in the air.

As promised by the instructor, the first approach by the student into the stage field was 'stair stepped'. Baker didn't say anything, but watched closely.

The student hovered to the panel for takeoff and the pattern was completed again. The second approach was the same. But, Baker had been watching. He had noticed the student had his head cocked down and to the left during the approach.

After the second approach, the student was told to hover the aircraft to the hardstand and shut it down. Baker took off his helmet and gloves, undid his seat belts and told the student to do the same.

Major Baker had the student show him where he was looking during the approach. After some time, the student determined he was looking down. Baker explained about using the peripheral vision during an approach and how to look for the panel without becoming fixed on it.

Two more approaches, and the student's problem was solved, Major Baker complimented him on each one, The student relaxed as if he had just been told that he won the Texas state lottery.

ii

Captain Richarde was working with his student, preparing him for the check ride that would have to be completed the next week. The student had been average, and hadn't presented any major problem.

Richarde's student had finally taken control of the helicopter after getting tired of looking at the Captain for help only to see the sign neatly-printed on the side of the instructors helmet; "What are you looking at me for dummy, DO SOMETHING!"

The student and Captain Richarde were on short final to the panel, It was to be an approach to the panel, instead of a hover. The student continued the approach past the three foot point, At that moment a gust of wind caught the TH55 helicopter.

Captain Richarde's student tried to correct, but over corrected, caught the left skid and bounced, striking the main rotor blade on the asphalt, The TH55 proceeded to thrash itself into little pieces as it settled to the ground, amidst a cloud of dust, never to rise again.

Major Baker was still with his 'prog ride', he heard the tower call, "all aircraft depart the stage field pattern, we have an accident", Baker looked at lane three, just in time to see a man built like an ice box step delicately out of the flying pieces of helicopter, turn gently on his toes, remove his helmet and slam it into the ground!

In spite of the accident, Baker had to laugh, he had just been told that morning that Bill Richarde only needed two and a half hours to get his 500 hour safety award. And, Bill had been flying only-one hour that day.

iii

Bubba Watkins had just turned fourteen the week before. His father bought him a bow and arrows for his birthday. He was spending Saturday afternoon in the hilly part of Palo Fin to county looking for something to try the arrows on.

Bubba was not retarded. But, he was a slow learner. He had his difficulties in school, and like many, would come out of it later. He was the butt of a. lot of jokes in his school, and in some eyes, was considered "the village idiot". He did have good mechanical aptitude, and he knew how to read.

The primary training at Fort Wolters involved cross country flights, night flying, slope landings, and mostly confined area, operations. Students were instructed how to get a helicopter into places that didn't seem large enough to make a landing. Often, during these trips into the hinterlands of Texas, a helicopter would become 'un-flyable', for one reason or another.

Late Friday afternoon, one of the primary students experienced a 'high frequency vibration' during his flight. The student landed the aircraft. His instructor made arrangements for the maintenance personnel to pick up the helicopter, and then flew the student back to the main airfield.

Maintenance received the report of the downed aircraft location. It was 4 P.M. The information was passed on to the relieving maintenance personnel. Later that night, the maintenance personnel would pick up the helicopter and return it for inspection. Somehow, the paperwork was misplaced.

Bubba was walking through a small mesquite growth, He was looking for a rabbit, an armadillo or anything to try his archery skill on. He looked up and saw it. A helicopter! He stopped and admired it, he had never seen one this close. At this point, if Bubba had filled the aluminum monster full of arrows, no one would have been surprised. But Bubba did something no one expected.

When the student left the aircraft, he forgot one important item. He forgot to take his check list for the helicopter. It was bound in a loose leaf binder. Bubba saw it immediately: It was hard to miss, it was bright orange with black printing, "PRE SOLO HELICOPTER TRAINING!".

The loose leaf binder contained everything and anything anyone needed to know about starting the helicopter. It contained step by step details for the pre-flight, precautions,, starting, takeoff and landings, An entire flight school, wrapped up in 40-50 pages. And, there was no one nearby to tell Bubba that he might be doing it wrong!

Bubba's lips were moving like a rapid fire machine gun as he leafed through the training manual, He had just set a new record in speed reading!

Bubba got into the helicopter, adjusted the seat as prescribed in the manual, put the shoulder harness on and clasped the seat belt in place, Now, all he had to do was find everything according to the manual.

After a few attempts to start the helicopter, to no avail, Bubba noticed the magneto switch, He reread the starting procedures and it said, "place the magneto switches on both, and engage starter", Oh well, if all else fails, read the instructions.

The engine cranked again and again, Still no start, Bubba paused momentarily and read back one page, "Advance engine cut off to full rich", Bubba pressed the start button again, Ah hah! It started!

The Bell OH13 sat there, engine chugging away, rotor blades turning, Bubba grinning. After some experimenting with the throttle control, the engine was running smoothly, and about 200 RPM's above the red line, Bubba, with all of his speed reading, hadn't got to the "My God don't do this" portion of the book.

Bubba pulled on the cyclic stick, nothing happened, except that the rotor blade plane tilted, He pulled up on the collective and the helicopter started to come off the ground. Bubba Pushed it back down quickly and sat there, thinking. So far, the thing in his left hand caused the helicopter to come off the ground, the thing in his right hand did nothing.

Bubba figured, "If I pull up on the thing in my left hand, then the helicopter will be off the ground and just sit there like they do on the television", Bubba pulled the thing in his left hand.

The helicopter came off the ground and rose, and rose, and rose, The nose tipped forward ever so slightly and Bubba was making a maximum, maximum performance take off just like the professionals.

'Yahoo!" Bubba yelled, as the helicopter continued to climb, and turn to the right, Bubba didn't know what to do to stop the turn, his hands were already full and he couldn't stop to read the manual again, The helicopter continued to turn, a little tighter until it was 300 feet in the air.

At first, Bubba thought, he hadn't had this much fun since he rode the 'octopus' at 'Six Flags over Texas', As the turns began to increase in velocity, Bubba suddenly realized he wasn't in an amusement park.

"Godamm" Bubba screamed as everything around him started turning to the soft brown stuff, He had run out of skill and ideas already, and had logged five minutes of flying time.

Finally Bubba released his death grip on the throttle control, the aircraft started down and the spinning slowed as the engine RPM's reduced.

Bubba still had the collective pitch up which slowed the descent, not enough to prevent the ultimate crash, but enough to keep the intrepid birdman on the earth's surface a while longer.

iv

"CHICKEN SHIT"", the class responded to Major Baker's daily query about the color of the Marine uniform. Major Baker made a few of the less important announcements and then announced who would be getting their check rides that day, As each name was called, there was a visible tremble as sweat broke out on the student's forehead. The tension was eased somewhat when Baker announced that Bubba Watkins would get his check ride that day.

The day would be easy for some of the flight instructor's, Several of the students would meet their "standardization pilot" at Downing AAF, then proceed to the stage field, One of each approach, takeoff and autorotation later, and they would be in calm seas, The instructor's for those students would drive out to the stage field and worry.

Many of the instructor's would drive to the stage field and sit in the sun to soak the booze out of their pores. The weekend hail and farewell had been a good one.

The Baker's had run out of booze for the Bombay punch at their house after the club party and everyone had contributed anything that remained in a. bottle, the concoction tasted horrible and hit the imbibers like a sledge hammer. All during the party, the wives were discussing the upcoming General's reception and still wondering whether it was going to be gloves, hat, hat and gloves or none of the above.

Major Baker would drive to Tuy Hoa stage field and get the tower opened and operational. Usually, within fifteen minutes, the aircraft would begin arriving for the period. Today, Baker wanted to get there early, he needed to call the Pentagon from the stage field phone.

Baker had been going to night school at the local colleges. In fact, he was going five days a week. Since his arrival at Ft. Wolters. he had upgraded his education considerably.

Baker had taken any and all end of course exams available, had gone to night school and managed to attain 24 semester hours of credit within the span of one year, It was nearly as much as a full time student could master, Baker also completed the G.E.D. series of tests, receiving a full two years credit for completion.

With one more semester. Baker would be eligible for the Army 'degree completion program', With six months or less to complete, the Army would send him to college and a degree.

The stage field was deserted, no helicopters yet. Baker picked up the phone and dialed the phone number for Artillery Branch at the Pentagon, The Lt, Colonel who answered was informed of who it was, and asked, "will I be here long enough to finish another semester?" Baker then related what he had accomplished and his desires regarding the degree program.

The Lieutenant Colonel said, "we were just getting ready to call you, You are scheduled for a second tour in Viet Nam". No matter what Baker said, he could not get the assignments officer to let him go to college first. Baker "was needed in Viet Nam, as soon as possible", Orders would be received within the week.

Baker sat quietly watching the traffic pattern begin to develop, He was thinking about what to say to his wife, what to do about selling his home, and last of all, about Viet Nam, Baker decided to tell his wife that weekend, after the General's reception.

V

"Tuy Hoa tower, this is Army 18421 departing for Downing", "Roger 421, have you departing". Baker replied as he scratched the aircraft number off the list, Captain Jimmy Simpson and the student had started back for the day.

Jimmy Simpson was the operations officer for the flight. He was a Texan. Jimmy commuted between Mineral Wells and Ft. Worth on a daily basis. Baker and Simpson had become good friends over the past years.

During the flight back and forth to the stage fields, the students were always tested for their abilities, in the event of an engine failure. The flight instructor would close the engine throttle down to idle and announce "forced landing", The student was then graded on his field selection, how quickly he started autorotation, and how well he managed the descent.

Jimmy had given the forced landing announcement. The student laid it out well, made a good field selection and was completing the procedure to take it all the way to the ground, when Jimmy said, "I've got the aircraft".

The student leaned back and relaxed as Jimmy debriefed him on the intercom concerning what he had done right and what he had done wrong, Instead of climbing out, Jimmy kept the helicopter low, as he talked to the student, Neither pilot nor student saw the telephone wires until the skids came into contact.

The wire hit the skid struts just below the aircraft fuselage causing the helicopter to tumble end over end through the air, Jimmy Simpson was dead on impact, the student survived with minor injuries, It would take several years for Major Baker to get over the loss of Jimmy.

The word finally arrived the morning of the General's reception. It was hat and gloves for the ladies. Major Baker had spent the early afternoon getting ready. The royal blue trousers with the wide gold piping and the dark blue tunic always looked good together, but it always gave Baker the irresistible urge to step out into the street to blow a whistle and yell 'taxi'.

Baker paced nervously as the time to depart approached. His wife had spent the morning getting a new hat and new white gloves for the affair. Finally, she said, "I'm ready!". Baker turned to look at her, and there she was with the cute little hat and the pretty white gloves, and that was all! Baker said, "they'll always remember us at Fort Wolters!".

vi

The orders arrived, Major Baker was to report to Ft. Rucker Alabama, TDY for training, to attend the flight instructor and the gunnery instructor's course for all Bell UH1 series aircraft, After completion he would attend the rotary wing instrument course.

Baker's orders went on to say that he would report to Travis AFB in Feb. 1370. A full six months away, The Army needed Baker in Viet Nam, "as soon as possible", but managed to put him in a temporary training status for six months at 20.00 a day per diem.

The trip to Dayton Ohio from Mineral Wells Texas was long and tiring. Baker was pulling his VW with the Buick station wagon, The VW was packed with immediate essentials for their arrival, plus a mother cat and four kittens. The car was packed with the Bakers.

During the trip to Dayton, Baker wondered if he hadn't made the call to the Pentagon, would he still be at Ft, Wolters? He was almost certain that his call had initiated the orders. The entire affair smelled of Marine green!

CHAPTER TEN

MAJOR BAKER SHIFTED in the seat, picked up another magazine and tried to get interested in it. It was a long flight from Travis AFB in California to Saigon.

Baker and his family had arrived in Dayton Ohio with cats, baggage and VW. They had purchased a home in the outskirts where the girls could attend a good school. This had been an easy move compared to many in the past. No house hunting.

After the 30 day leave, there were the parting tears, the nervous feeling about getting back into the combat zone and the promises of many letters. At least the family was settled nicely, one less-thing to worry about.

The trip to Viet Nam only took about 20 hours on the DCS compared to several days the first time. At least, the equipment was upgraded. The bad part, it gave the passengers arriving another two days in Viet Nam. The year started from the time they departed Travis.

After stops in Honolulu and Clark AFB in the Philippines, the big jet aircraft landed in Saigon. No ground fire this time, an easy flight all the way.

ii

Nothing had changed at Camp Alpha, they still had the same system. At least, they had replaced the tents with Quonset huts. Major Baker checked in, found out that they had him listed as AWOL due to a screw up in the paperwork, and found his quarters for the few nights he would be there. Now that he was a 'field grade officer', a little more time would be taken to determine his assignment.

Baker and another new arrival headed downtown to see the sights of Saigon. It still amazed Baker when he saw two Vietnamese men holding hands. His first inclination had been wrong, it was merely a. sign of good friendship.

The smells and the noise of Saigon had not changed. You could still smell the shit burning, mixed with the odors of cooking, petroleum and the musty dampness. The sound of horns from the mopeds, busses and jeeps was constant. The Vietnamese only knew of two controls when driving, the accelerator and the horn button.

The pair were accosted several times on the street by prostitutes, shoe shine boys and attempts to sell them marijuana. With very little effort, they could get serviced or high for several hundred Piasters, (ratio 100 to 1 dollar). If they used Military Payment Certificates (MPC), the cost was even less.

Military Payment Certificates was the legal form of currency for the military. The MPC notes came in 5, 10, 25 and 50 cent denominations as well as 1 dollar and five dollar notes. The MPC was exchanged for Piasters, which were used on the civilian market. A black market existed for a larger exchange rate of Piasters for MPC. But, the MPC were used for illegal activities.

Baker had seen MPC changed in a matter of hours by the U.S. Forces in Viet Nam. Leaves and passes were cancelled, a payroll officer arrived and old MPC notes were exchanged for new. The changes-were radical in the form of design and color.

When an exchange occurred, any MPC in the hands of civilians was worthless. The Vietnamese whores stood outside of the barbed wire of the military installations wailing, and, attempting to get the GI's to take their worthless MPC for new. Sometimes the exchange rate got as low as 25 cents on the dollar.

Baker and his companion caught a cab to the Army VIP flight detachment at the edge of Ton Son Nuht. This is where Bob would like to be assigned, and had plans to get the assignment. The hard stand had nothing but the best equipment. New fixed wing, new helicopters, and all plush with the best instruments and equipment.

Bob asked for the commanding officer. He was out of country, on R&R in Hong Kong. The executive officer was on a flight with a Brigadier General. Baker figured that he had a good chance of getting into one of the VIP flights because of his background. He would try again tomorrow.

Baker had been in a rough unit the first tour, and, from all that he heard, the assignments officers tried to give a plush job to the returnees with hard combat experience.

When Bob arrived at Camp Alpha he met a Ma.ior that was being assigned to Hong Kong as R&R officer because he was a returnee. Bob could picture himself in Tokyo. He decided he'd rent a small place and really enjoy himself for the year he would be there greeting the boys from Viet Nam.

iii

"Major Baker, you have a phone call", the message blared out over the camp speaker system. Baker came out of his daydream immediately and thought, hell I don't know anyone in camp, and it's too early for an assignment, I just arrived yesterday.

The assignments officer, on the other end of the phone, said, !'Are you trained in the AH1G cobra gunship?" Baker laughed into the mouthpiece, and replied, "hell no!" Baker felt he had them this time, now for the plush assignment.

The assignments officer didn't pause between sentences, and he didn't take a breath or stutter. "No problem we can get you trained in country in the cobra, and we need you right away in the 101st Airborne Division in Eye (I) Corps because of your experience in gunships pack your bags orders are enroute by courier".

Baker looked at the dead phone and wondered if it had been a. recording. It almost sounded like the Lt. Colonel from the Artillery branch at the Pentagon. Baker headed for the nearest latrine, and, he hadn't had a dapsone pill yet. This definitely smelled of Marine green, and it wasn't Baker's pants.

The orders arrived, as threatened. Not only was he assigned to the 101st Airborne Division, the orders specifically read, 4/77 FA (ARA). He was going to be assigned to an Aerial Rocket Artillery Battalion. Well, at least he would be in his branch this time.

At Hue Phu Bai, a jeep met Major Baker at the airfield. It was from the 4/77th FA (ARA), he was expected. Once he signed in and turned all of his records over to the personnel officer, Baker was summoned to the Battalion Commander's office.

Major Baker took an immediate liking to LTC Ray-Parton. He was easy going friendly, and seemed to have it all together. LTC Parton told Baker that he would be the new Battery Commander for C Battery. While checking Bob's form 66. LTC Parton noticed that Baker had been in the instructor end of the flying for the past two and a half years. "Baker, when you go to Vung Tau for the in-country-training in the cobra, try to get instructor rated in it. We need someone around here to give 90 day-check rides".

Baker spent the first two days at Battalion before heading 29 miles north to the location of his unit. While Baker finished his in-processing, he had a chance to see how different things were from his first tour. The battalion had a decent mess hall, permanent type quarters for the officers, and a real, honest to God, Officer's Club. He couldn't believe it. At least, it was going to be a little more pleasant.

The trip to Camp Evans in the UH1D only took a few minutes. He had arrived! The unit lay out was good. Permanent buildings, permanent mess hall, a small theater for movies, but no officer's club. Major Baker was introduced to the First Sergeant, the Executive Officer, Operations Officer and present unit commander. Baker would understudy the outgoing unit commander for two weeks before heading for Vung Tau.

The battery consisted of fifteen officer and warrant officer pilots, 120 enlisted personnel, and a maintenance unit attached to service the cobra. There were six cobras assigned to the unit.

The gunship unit kept a 'hot section' available on the pad at all times. The two aircraft were always ready to launch when a call came through for a 'fire mission'. Pilots were never very far from the aircraft, sleeping in a small hooch near the aircraft at night.

The section was required to be airborne in two minutes, and en route to their target area, Each aircraft carried 75 rockets on the short stubby wings, 250 rounds of 40mm and 2500 rounds of 7.62mm machine gun ammunition for the mini-gun in the turret, The mini-gun was capable of firing 2,000 or 4,000 rounds per minute depending upon the pilots desires.

Major Bob Baker's battery was referred to as the 'Griffins', a mythical animal with the body and hind legs of a lion, and the head and wings of an eagle, The battery had printed thousands of calling cards to be passed out to the infantry, who, in turn, placed them on the bodies of the enemy that were killed by the battery. The card read, "Love by Nature, Live by Luck, Kill by profession, Death on Call, wire Griffin, San Francisco 96383." The printing surrounded a picture of the Griffin.

Captain Bill Blair had just become the new executive officer for the Griffins. He would be in command temporarily while Baker completed his in country transition into the cobra, Blair was a graduate of West Point. Easy going, but efficient, Blair had a great sense of humor and reminded Baker of Jack Benny.

Camp Evans was located north of the Imperial City of Hue, The camp was in Quang Tri Province and just a few miles short of the DMZ that separated north and south Viet Nam. Because of this proximity, the Griffins had plenty of targets-available to them.

Unlike the Troop that Baker had been accustomed to the first tour, ARA was dedicated to support missions. All the firing missions would be at enemy concentrations located by other units of the 101st Division, Special Forces, the Australians or the 1/5th Mechanized Division on the DMZ, The Griffins did not go out to reconnoiter.

Major Baker began flying missions with the Griffins almost as soon as he arrived, Although not yet transitioned in the cobra, he rode in the front seat and became familiar with the missions the unit flew along with the armament in the front seat.

The front seat, co-pilot position, was in front of the pilot and a. couple of feet lower, The co-pilot gunner position had limited instruments-available, a very short collective stick on the left console and a short cyclic stick on the right console.

The aircraft was flown from the front with wrist action, A gunners sight located in the front seat operated the turret under the aircraft. With some improvement, the turret moved 90 degrees left and right, 110 degrees down and 45 degrees up. (the up movement was limited to preclude blowing the rotor blades off).

Baker had flown a few missions with the Griffins before he departed for Vung Tau. One evening, he received a call from Battalion headquarters. The battalion commander called to tell Baker he heard that Bob had been flying. Further, that he was not to fly missions on a daily basis in the future. Baker's primary job was to command. LTC Parton also wanted Baker available when he needed him. Baker let out a sigh of relief.

V

After his indoctrination with the Griffins, Baker departed for Vung Tau. Vung Tau is on the southernmost tip of South Viet Nam. The area had a heavy French influence left over from the days of the French Indo China era, It was on the coast, where the waters of the South China Sea and the Gulf of Siam met.

At one time, Vung Tau had been the French Riviera of Southeast Asia. It had a beautiful beach and the people were different. There was a lot of French blood in the citizens of Vung Tau, The people were less oriental and more French, Compared to what Baker had seen in other areas, the girls of Vung Tau had some beauty.

Baker couldn't believe it. Here was another one of those inequities that he had been encountering in Viet Nam. The group that conducted in-country training at Vung Tau was all military. They were living in stateside type conditions with air conditioning, good food, clubs, a beach and plenty of feminine companionship. And yet. they received the same credit as Baker for a Viet Nam tour.

vi

Baker loved to fly. especially helicopters. He had encountered his second love, the AHiG Cobra gunship. During the early years of Viet Nam. the UHI series Bell helicopter had been built for utility. It was not designed to become a gunship, but through good American inventiveness, it proved to be quite capable in that capacity.

The AHIG was the first helicopter designed and produced by Bell for the Viet Nam war as an attack helicopter.

The helicopter fuselage was narrow, just enough to permit a little shoulder room for the pilot or co-pilot in the tandem arrangement. The big Lycoming engine drove a forty eight foot rotor blade which was nearly thirty six inches wide. The helicopter had two hydraulic systems to give the power assist necessary to control the blades and a back up gas system available in the event the other two systems were damaged by gunfire.

Because of the size of the rotor system., the aircraft also had a SAS (Stabilization Augmentation System), The SAS provided assistance for pitch, roll and yaw. Without it, the aircraft was nearly uncontrollable at a hover.

The pilots seat was a mass of armor on both sides and under. The instrument panel afforded every instrument needed and then some, with all of the available instrument approach capabilities, plus back ups. Both left and right consoles were loaded with armament switches and various radio capabilities for any and all frequencies, to include secure scramblers, This arc raft actually looked like a fighter plane, It had one switch that Baker became extremely fond of, The ECU.

The ECU switch turned on the 'environmental control unit', It was an air conditioner. The aircraft needed it. Both pilot and co-pilot were under a hinged hatch that pulled down and locked, It was clear plastic from the front cockpit to the back, Without the ECU, the inside of the aircraft would get to as much as 120 degrees, When the ECU worked, it actually spit little snow flakes out of the ports.

The purpose of an orientation ride is to show any new pilot the training area. It also serves to familiarize him with the radio frequencies and other necessary information. After fifteen minutes into the orientation ride at the USARV standardization board school, the instructor asked Baker if he would like to try to fly the Cobra from the front seat.

Major Baker took the small controls, and did a few turns and then headed towards the USARV pad, The instructor said, "let's see if you can make a decent approach from the front". Baker set the approach up and began going through the MOI (methods of instruction) on the intercom.

"This is a normal approach of about twenty degrees, Once I reach my sight picture, I will gently lower the collective and start slowing the aircraft with the cyclic".

After a couple of approaches, the instructor said, "it's obvious that you have been doing some instructing, let me see you do a touch down autorotation". Baker started the traffic pattern and thought about the construction of the cobra, He was well forward of the skids and the sight picture for an autorotation was going to be quite different. Always before, he was sitting over the skids., the front seat had definite disadvantages.

The cobra was lined up, the power rolled off to idle position and the collective lowered gently, Baker called out on the intercom, "rotors in the green, lined up!" "Rotor RPM getting a little high, collective coming in," Baker added a little pitch to the blades to bring the needle down for the rotor RPM's then quickly lowered it again, The rotor RPM's stabilized in the green arc.

"Fifty feet from touchdown, slowing the aircraft with cyclic", Baker came back on the short stubby little stick on the right console bringing the nose of the helicopter up and at the same time slowing the forward speed, The giant rotor immediately brought the helicopter to a walk, Baker held it a little longer to lose some of the altitude before leveling the aircraft right at the point of zero forward movement, "Corning in with collective. Baker called out", The cobra sat down on the grass strip with little or no forward movement and a gentle rocking.

After landing, the USARV standardization instructor told Baker that he had never seen anyone make a touchdown autorotation from the front seat of a. cobra before and had only let Baker try it because he handled the aircraft so well from the front, Just like Bubba, Baker grinned.

For some unknown reason, Baker had an innate understanding of helicopters, He always seemed to understand them, During his TDY instructor training at Ft, Rucker, the Warrant Officer standardization instructor had told that he had never seen anyone with Baker's feel and innate understanding of how an autorotation should be accomplished.

The USARV instructor pilot at Vung Tau told the detachment flight commander that Baker should in the front seat and graduate as an instructor, rather than pilot, That accomplished, Baker continued with the week long course in preparation for his return to Hue Phu Bai.

Like any aircraft, the cobra had it's bad features, A total loss of hydraulics could be a real disaster, Although Baker had not experienced it, the controls were almost impossible to move in the event the hydraulic assist was not available.

Because of this. Bell had a second hydraulic system, And, a gas system in the event the primary and the secondary systems were gone, The gas system would permit the pilot to move the collective fully up and down three times only, Making an approach without some sort of assist on the collective was nearly impossible.

There were also rumors that the blade would flex down through the front cockpit in the event of a hard landing, When this happened, the 36 inch mass of aluminum, with the steel leading edge, could pass through the front cockpit. From all rumors, if it happened, the co-pilot/instructor became an immediate candidate to sell peanuts to the midgets at the circus.

The situation for Baker had come full about. In this tour, he was going to be out front of the pilot, and under the swinging aluminum saber every time he gave a check ride, He would have to learn to shrink!

Before his return to Phu Bai, Baker had a chance to experience the beach of Vung Tau, It was beautiful. The waters were pleasant, and the girls were great to look at, It was to be short lived however, Baker would return to Phu Bai the next day.

vii

Baker received the call from Phu Bai. A new cobra just arrived in the Vung Tau port. The Battalion commander wanted Baker to fly it back to the 4/77th ARA, Baker had no gun, no charts and very few minutes in the back seat of the cobra. On top of it all, this cobra was brand new and not yet proven that it would run consistently and forever!

Early the next day, Baker left Vung Tau en route to Hue Phu Bai in the cobra. The trip was a little over a thousand miles from the very tip of South Viet Nam to the DMZ (demilitarized zone), Baker didn't have frequencies, charts, gun or any great desire to fly over open enemy territory in an unarmed and brand new helicopter. He didn't even know where the enroute refueling points were.

Baker stayed on the emergency frequency and decided to use it, no matter what. He lifted off from Vung Tau heading for the coastline, If nothing else, he could keep the blue of the ocean on the right and the green of the jungle on the left tracking the coastline north.

After two hours of flying. Baker received the call on his emergency frequency (UHF 243.0). "Aircraft flying north along the coastline, this is central control," Baker acknowledged the call. "Roger Army 98455. we have a battleship that is firing on a coastline target, make an immediate right turn to 090 degrees!". Baker complied, made a right turn, and headed out into the South China Sea.

Baker kept looking over his shoulder as the coastline disappeared behind him. Ten minutes, then fifteen minutes passed. Baker lacked two other pieces of equipment. A life vest, and the ability to swim. He had snookered his way through the Navy and a year at sea without learning.

Baker finally called central control and told them he was turning back because of his inability to breath under water. "Roger Army 455, we sort of forgot about you!". Great, thought Baker, Baker requested the nearest refueling place and radio frequency. Central control complied with the frequency and the Air Force Base at Tuy Hoa as the nearest "fuel. Baker was beginning to feel it was old home week.

The Air Force base was new at Tuy Hoa, At least, it was new since Baker's last visit with the 1/9th. After landing, the helicopter was shut down. A fuel truck rolled up with a fresh transfusion of JP-4, The Air Force personnel had not seen a cobra helicopter before, so Baker spent some time showing it to those that arrived at the aircraft, After taking on a full 1,200 pounds of the fuel in preparation for the last leg of the journey, Baker lifted off.

Once he broke ground at Tuy Hoa, the Air Force tower asked Baker for a low pass. Baker brought the cobra around, then made a steep dive to nearly 200 knots at runway altitude with a beautiful cyclic climb and turn toward his route of travel. Green on the left, blue on the right.

CHAPTER ELEVEN

IT WAS BARELY the year of the dog' after Baker arrived back in Phu Bai. He was told by the Battalion Commander that the new cobra gunship was his, received a last minute briefing, and left for Camp Evans and his new assignment as Battery Commander.

Once in the battery, Baker was to find his home away from home. In the beginning, he had feared the responsibility of command. Soon, he would begin to love it, He was miles from 'the flagpole' of the Battalion and enjoyed the challenge the job presented.

Baker would have some problems to deal with, He had a Lieutenant that had been grounded for coming too close to the grandstands holding infantry troops during a firing demonstration.

The lieutenant had not come close with rockets, After the firing demonstration, he had decided to show the troops a low pass near the grandstands. He got a little closer than intended and hit the stands with the aircraft. That was right after the troops had parted company with their seats.

Because of the nature of the ARA, the enlisted personnel were not used on combat missions, The cobra was a two man aircraft only, and it called for a pilot and co-pilot/gunner.

The enlisted personnel were in support assignments only. Each cobra had a crew chief and a weapons specialist. The remainder of the personnel were used for refueling, rearming, clerical and general support functions, Other than an occasional guard duty tour on the Camp perimeter, the enlisted personnel had a lot of free time on their hands.

Because of the free time, there were some problems with boredom. Something that Baker had not encountered during his first tour. The troops had access to the theater tent, beer and there was the availability of drugs. Baker was beginning to find the problem children of the unit and would have a few difficulties to keep him busy.

The drug amnesty program had been initiated in Viet Nam during Baker's second tour. Persons that had a problem could talk to the Commanding Officer about their difficulties, be referred to the hospital for help, and not have to worry about reprisal.

SP4 Ferryman approached Major Baker's desk, saluted and asked if he could have a private conversation with Baker. Baker closed the door to his office and listened. Ferryman admitted to having a real drug problem, and he wanted help, The young black enlisted man was even having some difficulty talking, and obviously strung out during his conversation with Baker.

Baker assured Ferryman of his support and made the necessary arrangements for his hospital stay at Camp Evans, Perryman departed that day for the cure.

ii

Lt. Dick Fairchild had been with the Griffins at Camp Evans for nearly two years when Major Baker arrived. Fairchild arrived as a WO-1 shortly-after flight school. After his tour was up, he had extended for six months, then six more. Each time Fairchild extended, he took the 30 day free leave, flew home to Florida and then returned, ready to do more battle.

Fairchild had applied for the direct commission that was offered to the Warrant Officers during Viet Nam. Because of his time in the Army, he received a direct appointment to 1st Lieutenant. Fairchild was nearing the end of his second extension and considering a third when Baker arrived.

During Fairchild's last trip to Florida, between extensions, he had worn a captured NVA officer's uniform to the bank in his hometown, The uniform didn't fit well, and was covered with dried blood.

Fairchild had killed the previous owner of the uniform and felt some compulsion to wear it while home. Baker decided that Fairchild would bear close watching.

Fairchild was always first to volunteer for any mission that was considered more dangerous then normal. Because of his desire to fly the tough missions, he already had been awarded several silver stars and a purple heart.

iii

Shortly after Baker's arrival in the battery, he was flying a mission with one of his officer's. Baker was flying the aircraft from the back seat. The officer in the front seat had been with the unit for a while and was showing some of the unit locations to the commanding officer.

The infantry unit requested a fire mission from the ARA Battalion, and the Griffins responded. The U.S. unit was on a ridge line running north and south with the enemy in the slight draw below them. Baker flew the aircraft while the gunner fired 40mm at the enemy unit. During the final pass, as Baker started his turn towards the enemy position, the infantry unit radioed that they were receiving "the gunships 40 mike mike fire., with several wounded".

The turret had malfunctioned. The co-pilot gunner reported after he had started firing, the turret suddenly slew to the left, throwing rounds up on the ridge where the friendly troops were located. Even though the trigger was released immediately, the gun continued to fire. Baker was totally unaware of what had happened until it was over.

The battalion appointed investigating officer, Major Lynn, arrived at Camp Evans the following day. Any time a 'friendly fire incident' occurred, a complete investigation was required.

The investigating officer was the Battery Commander from A battery, of the ARA unit. He talked to Major Baker and the officer that had been operating the turret, Even though he was told about the turret problem, he appeared to direct his investigation towards ineptitude on the part of the crew.

When the investigation results were shown to Major Baker, the investigating officer had taken the easy way out by making it appear that the gunner and Major Baker had caused the incident.

Upon reading the results. Baker got in touch with the in-country manufacturer's representative for the turret company, The civilian from the company arrived at Camp Evans and pronounced that the turret had malfunctioned, locating the part (a limiter switch) that had failed.

The new evidence was provided to the battalion, and Baker and the gunner were cleared of any failure on their part. Baker hoped that the Major who investigated the incident would eventually present the right opportunity in the future. Baker vowed to clean his clock.

iv

The special forces unit in the tri-border area had requested a fire mission. They had troops in the open with five ton Russian trucks. The tri-border area was just north of Camp Evans where Laos, South Viet Nam and North Viet Nam joined.

A heavy section (3) of cobras responded to the call, The special forces personnel were contacted and the location of the trucks was given to the Pilots. The trucks were just off of a narrow road, under some trees.

As the noisy cobras approached at full speed, the NVA soldiers broke from cover, running to the trucks in an attempt to get them out of the area so they wouldn't be destroyed.

The first cobra, to roll in on the running NVA's was carrying flechette rockets. The pilot fired 8 pair of the nail bearing rockets and pinned the NVA troops to anything near them. The next two cobras finished the job by destroying the trucks.

The cobra's carried flechette rockets on at least one of the aircraft in the hot section, The warhead of the rocket contained 2200 small nails with fins. At a certain distance from the target, the base detonating explosive in the warhead would open the container and the nails would splay out. The small nails would stabilize, hitting the target at better than 2,000 foot per second.

The special forces troops moved into the area after the trucks were destroyed to pick up any weapons or intelligence. The NVA troops were found nailed to the surrounding trees. Some weapons were even nailed to trees. The Griffins were credited with 22 kills and five trucks.

V

Major Baker and his executive officer, Captain Blair, began flying together in the same aircraft when the opportunity presented itself. Often, they would tag along with the 'hot section' to observe, or join in when needed.

The call for a 'fire mission' had come from a lone Australian infantryman north of the Ashau valley. The 'Aussie' had a large platoon of South Vietnamese ARVN troops with him, and they were in heavy contact with the enemy. The hot section plus Major Baker and Captain Blair lifted off to the coordinates provided by the Battalion.

The location of the friendly troops was a small finger of high land sticking out into a valley that was the extension of the Ashau. The Ashau was known to be heavily concentrated with enemy troops. Heavy equipment movement and large troop concentrations had been observed in the valley at night.

The heavy section arrived at the location of the Australian. He popped smoke to show his location on the finger of land and indicated that the enemy troops were at the far tip. The three gunships fired 20 rockets from each ship into the location indicated and were told that the enemy troops had been killed or repelled. End of mission, time to return to Camp Evans.

While the gunships were in the valley, heavy fog had begun to form, Attempts to reverse the course to Evans failed because all of the connecting valleys had closed up with dense fog, The three cobras tried a northern route and found themselves in a box canyon with barely enough room to turn around while at a hover.

After some radio discussion, Lt Fairchild decided that he wanted to climb out on top of the fog and head towards the South China Sea to look for a break in the fog. The other two cobra's decided to chance the southern route through the Ashau.

The two cobra gunships started south in the valley opening into the Ashau. Once the valley opened up into the large Ashau itself, both cobras dropped to ground level, pulling as much power as possible.

At top speed, the two gunships pulled abreast of each other, Both pilots had armed the weapons system and had their fingers on the trigger. The enemy troops that were in the valley were startled or asleep, both cobras moving through the area at maximum speed sounded like diesel freight trains at IBS MPH. Although expected, no enemy fire was received as the two ships moved through the area.

vi

It was payday, Major Baker was making the monthly payroll to the enlisted troops as they lined up outside of the hooch that was Baker's office as well as the offices for the executive officer and battery personnel clerks, Each name was checked off the list by

Captain Blair, the man would report to Major Baker and he would count the money out.

"Incoming", the troops hit the ground all around the hooch, Major Baker and Captain Blair joined the clerk typists Jordan and Kraft, As they lay there, all of them laughed, A nervous reaction. The enemy harassment was over within a few minutes, no damage to the battery area, and payday was resumed. The mortar rounds were frequent, sometimes during the day and sometimes at night.

The black SFC reported to Major Baker and said, "Sir, the black enlisted personnel want to have a meeting with you to express their grievances about the way they are being treated", Baker set the time for 1300 hours, in the theater tent.

Just before and during lunch Baker did some checking to find out what may have caused the problem, Nothing could be found except for one thing. The battery drunk, a black sergeant, had convinced the rest of the black troops that they were being mistreated and had managed to get them together and behind a confrontation with Major Baker.

Baker was well aware of the Sgt. as an agitator and potential trouble maker. The sergeant had caused previous problems because of his drinking.

Baker decided to gamble on common sense during the meeting.

Major Baker was sitting on the stage smoking a cigarette when the troops filed in at the rear of the tent. The SFC seemed reluctant when he said, "Sir, the troops feel that they have a grievance, Sergeant Walls is their spokesman".

The alcoholic sergeant started talking, His speech pattern was not only slurred by alcohol, he was using the black lingo that he felt would impress the troops. He was waving his arms and making little sense. "We aint gettin no mother fuckin help from battalion on this". "The fust sarge don pay no mothu fuckin tention ".

Baker listened, and after a few minutes, stood up, "Hold it right there!", Baker said. "Now if you feel that you have a grievance, I want to know about it", "Only one thing, you are going to have an interpreter for me, because I don't understand one damned thing that mother is saying!".

There was a moment of silence, and then they started laughing, Before long, they were all looking at the sergeant and laughing, Soon, they all filed out of the tent, The alcoholic sergeant turned and left.

That afternoon six of the enlisted personnel approached Major Baker and told him that they wanted to be transferred with him when it was time for him to leave. One individual went as far as to tell the Battalion Commander that Major Baker was the "only white man he had ever respected".

Major Baker contacted the black SFC that had made arrangements for the meeting. The SFC admitted that there weren't any real problems and that Baker's method had got everyone's attention.

vii

The mission didn't require the 'hot section', It was simple escort of a large Chinook helicopter making an ammunition delivery to the firebase in the valley north of the Ashau. The firebase was the home of a 155mm artillery unit. The Chinook would sling load a large quantity of artillery ammunition into the ammunition bunker.

Baker and Blair along with a cobra being flown by Lt, Bailey and his co-pilot, stayed on each side of the Chinook for protection as it hovered in over the ammunition storage area and released it's load of ammunition. The ammunition handlers on the ground guided the big pallets of ammo into their proper place. Each time the handlers would make the signal for the release and the Chinook would depart for another load.

The third load was on it's way in, The cobras set up a pattern to stay on each side of the big helicopter, The Chinook approached the ammunition dump and started to hover in over the handlers.

Baker just started his break to the right when he saw the machine gun fire hit the engine compartment of the Chinook helicopter. The big aircraft burst into flames immediately, and started settling down into the hug pile of powder bags, projectiles and other ammunition.

Within seconds, the helicopter exploded, The ammunition dump was burning, exploding, and throwing unexploded artillery rounds all over the firebase. At the same time, the enemy unit nearby began lobbing mortar rounds into the firebase.

The enemy had taken advantage of the opportunity, Following the direct hit on the helicopter, they started firing the mortar rounds and began moving infantry in for an assault on the hill.

In just a few minutes, it seemed to Baker, the decision was made to retrograde from the firebase, The unit would be removed immediately while the firebase was under fire. Lift ships began arriving, and troops were moved off of the fire base while support from the cobra gunships continued.

The cobras from the Griffins looked for targets of opportunity in the valley below the firebase. The Air Force had been called for additional support and was directed in to targets for the 500 pound bombs they carried.

Baker and Blair were at about 800 feet when they felt the aircraft pitch and nearly roll over, A F-100 had just flown under them, climbed out and released it's 500 pound 'high drag' bomb. The bomb floated lazily in front of the cobra, as it slowly arced upwards before starting the descent to the target below.

Within two hours, the fireba.se was completely evacuated of all personnel, The aircraft were still looking for targets when a red smoke grenade popped on top of the firsbase. Close examination revealed one lone soldier who had been left behind. The lift ship was called back and he was removed to safer territory.

viii

Major Baker and Captain Blair had taken on two other officers in a pinochle game in Baker's hooch, It had been an ongoing challenge for over a month now, with return matches, Baker and Blair had consistently won the other two officer's paychecks and were in the process of lining their pockets again, when the field phone rang.

It was the hospital, SP4 Ferryman had walked out of the hospital. When he walked out, he mentioned that he was "going to see Major Baker!", The hospital had called because they felt that Ferryman meant harm, There had been cases of officers being 'fragged' in Viet Nam by enlisted personnel when they felt disgruntled, They would open a tent flap or door and pitch a grenade in with the officer.

Concentration on the pinochle game was difficult, The other players had been told of the call, and they continued to play.

The door to the hooch flew open, and in walked Ferryman. Baker continued to look at his cards, looked up casually, and said. "I thought you were in the hospital!" Ferryman said, "I got tired of the hospital and decided to see you!" Ferryman walked the length of the hooch and stood next to Baker, and asked, "What are you doing?" Baker replied, "playing pinochle", Baker proceeded to explain the game, and then said, "You look tired Ferryman, why don't you go to your hooch and go to bed, I'll talk to you tomorrow". Ferryman nodded, and left, By this time, the other three players had turned blue from holding their breath.

ix

"LTC Parton wants to see you", Baker hung up the field phone in his hooch and wondered what that was all about, He had not had any recent problems that required a dressing down by the Battalion Commander, Baker informed his executive officer of his departure for Battalion and headed for his cobra on the flight line.

LTC Ray Parton looked at Major Baker as he saluted and reported, Parton smiled and said, "Bob, we are going to have a hail and farewell at the officer's club this month." "I just discovered that there is a navy hospital ship laying at anchor in the South China Sea." "From your records I notice that you were in the navy. Do you think you could fly out there and get some nurses to attend our party?".

Baker couldn't believe it. He hadn't been aboard a Navy ship since his discharge from the Navy, Now, 20 years later, he was going to be doing a first, he was going to land on one.

X

Baker made arrangements to fly out in the Battalion's UHIH helicopter, Larger than the UHI's that he had flown before, they were capable of carrying fourteen passengers plus crew.

Since Baker had been in the Navy, he would make the first approach to the pad on the pitching deck and give the co-pilot a ship landing check out at the same time, Other than understanding the LSO (landing signal officer) on the pad, it wouldn't be very difficult.

"Roger Army 183392, this is the LSO, make your approach from the starboard quarter, winds are 110 degrees at 12 knots, seas are calm!" Baker made the approach into the pad from the right rear portion of the ship explaining each portion of it to the co-pilot, Major Lynn. Major Lynn, 'A' battery commander would drop Baker off and then return later after the arrangements were made.

Baker alighted from the helicopter, and as it lifted off to return to the Battalion to await his call, Baker turned, saluted the colors and then saluted the deck officer, "Requesting permission to come aboard sir". The Navy Lieutenant returned the salute, said "permission granted", and asked the nature of the call. Baker said, "I am requesting permission to speak to your captain".

Major Baker was shown into the Captain's quarters, saluted the Navy Captain and was offered a. chair at the table with the linen table cloth. The captain said, "would you like coffee?", Baker said, "of course". Presently, the Philippino stewards mate appeared with the silver server and fine china cups. Baker thought to himself, well at least I made it on a temporary basis.

After offering the invitation to the Captain to attend the party on shore, along with 25 of his best looking nurses, Baker and the captain sat and talked. Baker was enjoying his time in the sun. An agreement had been reached, and two helicopters from the battalion would arrive the next Friday night to retrieve their precious cargo.

The Friday night party was a success. All of the nurses and the Hospital Ship Captain enjoyed the chance to get ashore and see how the Army lived. After the party, they had been safely returned to the ship. Now it was time to pay a call to the ship Captain to thank him for his cooperation.

Major Lynn requested permission to go with Major Baker when he paid his respects to the Hospital Ship Captain, both were flown the the ship and deposited on the helicopter pad, The ground swells were more evident, and the ship, laying at anchor, was rocking gently from port to starboard.

After the courtesy call had been completed, and the helicopter summoned for the pickup, Major Baker and Major Lynn stood on the ship's bridge to watch for the UH1H to return, The bridge was one deck higher and the ground swells more accentuated at that point.

Baker stood talking to Major Lynn and watched as his face started turning a slight, but noticeable shade of green. As they talked, Bob also noticed the sweat beginning to pop out on Major Lynn's upper lip. Baker began to sway a little more from right to left as he continued to talk to Lynn, The greener Lynn's complexion became, the more Major Baker swayed.

Baker laughed to himself as Lynn lay on the floor of the helicopter, his head hanging out of the door. Lynn had already lost his hat and his sun glasses and now he was violently losing lunch. Baker thought, "puke you son of a bitch, that will teach you to try to make me look bad on that friendly fire incident".

From that day on. whenever he could, Baker would stand and sway, ever so slightly, while talking to Major Lynn, and the Major would blow lunch.

CHAPTER TWELVE

L T, FAIRCHILD AND his chase cobra were returning from an escort mission, The mission had lasted less than 30 minutes with no enemy contact. Fairchild's aircraft was still fully loaded with the seventy-six flechette rockets.

The escort mission had taken the two cobras into a canyon south of the Ashau valley and west of Camp Evans. It was a clear day. Lt. Fairchild decided to drop down for a tree skimming, low level flight, out of the canyon.

As the two cobras skimmed along at 160 knots, they turned, climbed and descended in order to stay just above the trees as they headed east.

Just as they crested a small hill, Fairchild saw them. The NVA company size unit was in the middle of an abandoned air strip, in full uniform. The Lieutenant couldn't believe his eyes. It appeared to be a marshaling area in preparation for battle.

In the split second it took Fairchild to recognize the enemy force, he reached up with his left hand and switched the small pointer on the selector to 'salvo'. As he pressed the firing button under his right thumb, the rockets began leaving the four pods arranged under the stubby wings of the cobra.

The entire 76 rockets were firing at the rate of one rocket every sixth of a second. The entire load of finishing nails would be spread the full length of the runway. As the rocket motors burned out, the base detonating fuse opened the warheads and displayed a small puff of red chalk dust to let the pilot know they had activated.

Fairchild could see the string of red puffs as each rocket splayed the nails out. To the pilot, the entire load of rockets seemed to take forever. As he got closer to the target, he could see the NVA soldiers folding. It almost appeared as if he was mowing wheat. The one hundred plus kills had taken a little less than thirteen seconds.

It took Fairchild much longer than thirteen seconds to get over the short battle. For days, he would talk about it in the mess hall, his eyes would glaze over and he would nearly froth at the mouth. Fairchild returned to the United States within a month of the large kill and Baker would always wonder what he did for a living.

ii

Major Baker and Captain Blair had been on an escort mission. They too returned with a full armament load. Before returning to the Griffin pad, the cobra needed to be refueled.

Captain Blair was flying from the back seat, He made his approach into the refueling area which ran north and south and contained no less than twenty nozzles for the thirsty aircraft. The area was narrow and perhaps 200 feet long.

The aircraft touched down on the far edge of the narrow portion of the refueling point. Blair dismounted from the back seat while Baker kept his hands on the controls, to prevent creep. It was

a. hot day, and they were going to have to take off downwind. All incoming traffic was landing behind them.

As soon as the gauge indicated 1,000 pounds of fuel, Baker motioned for Blair to shut it off. The captain replaced the nozzle and climbed the two steps on the fuselage to get into the rear cockpit.

Baker relaxed as the hatch was closed and locked, he watched the instruments as Blair rolled the power up to 6,000 RPM then used the governor increase switch to move the RPM's to 6600. Blair called out 'clear left, clear right' as Baker turned, looked and repeated 'clear left, clear right'.

Captain Blair pulled the aircraft to a hover and added forward cyclic to get the aircraft into translational lift. The cobra moved forward five feet and then started sinking just as the low RPM warning horn started blaring and the lights started blinking.

From the edge of the refueling point forward, in the direction of takeoff, were a large number of ammunition bunkers. The area around the bunkers consisted of ditches, holes, small hills and no open areas to make a touchdown.

The aircraft was already too low. To lower the collective in order to regain engine RPM's would result in ground contact, on a possible ammunition storage area.

By this time, Baker had said. "I have the aircraft", As an instructor pilot in the cobra, he was going to be responsible for whatever the results were, he may as well try to save it.

The cobra started turning slowly to the right, Because of the low RPM's, effective tail rotor control was being lost. The fuselage was beginning to turn in the opposite direction of the rotor system. Baker held the little bit of altitude and tried to squeeze more power in. There wasn't any power left.

The turns were starting to get tighter, as the fuselage spun to the right. The aircraft was slowly moving over the holes, hills and ammunition supply points. Baker was beginning to feel like Bubba Watkins in Texas, but he wasn't grinning!

Baker could see a. narrow road that adjoined one of the troop areas. It was just beyond the ammunition areas, and flat! Slowly, he was moving that way.

Swish, Baker caught a glimpse of the refueling point they just left, swish, there was the narrow road, getting closer, The ride was like something out of Disneyland, with no admission fee.

With a lot of luck, and some skill, Baker managed to get the aircraft perpendicular to the road at the exact right time. At that point, he rolled off all of the power. The cobra stopped the violent spinning almost immediately.

As the aircraft swung into alignment with the road and settled, Baker pulled all of what remained of the pitch in the blades. The skids folded up nicely to the fuselage as the aircraft struck the ground. Baker thought, they may be all bent to hell, but it will make it easier for Blair to get out to check his shorts.

Baker sat in the front seat of the aircraft watching the big rotor blades bounce up, then down as they continued to rotate. The major was doing his shrinking act in the front seat as the rotor system came close to reducing his height to five foot, four inches.

After the blades stopped turning, Captain Blair stepped out of the aircraft, walked around to the front, looked at Major Baker, saluted and shrugged one of his Jack Benny looks. Baker shook his head and gave the international 'so what' gesture.

iii

The new Battalion Commander arrived the week before, His name was LTC Charles Novak, He assumed command from LTC Ray Parton and began making a tour of his batteries.

The 'Griffins' were scheduled for their visit from the battalion CO the next day. The battery area was cleaned, and all personnel were alerted to the visit, Just a few things needed final adjustment before the Battalion Commander's arrival.

Baker checked in to his operations bunker and removed the 'GOD' from the top of the clear plastic board, and replaced it with his name, His operations officer had a sense of humor at least, The board contained the names of the pilots, their flying time, credited kills and other pertinent information, The battery had accumulated over 800 confirmed kills. When Baker arrived, the number was a little over 300.

The UH1H made the approach to the Griffin pad and shut down, Major Baker was waiting for the new CO with his jeep and driver, As the LTC approached, Baker saluted and introduced himself, The LTC didn't smile and said little, Baker began getting a little concerned, he had it easy when LTC Parton was in command. This looked like a different ball game.

Baker showed the new Battalion Commander the hot spot, the separated parking area for the other cobras, and then the maintenance facility. As they drove towards the mess hall, the Lieutenant Colonel said, "I've seen enough, take me to my aircraft," Baker was really concerned now, the new LTC had only been there 15 minutes.

As the Lieutenant Colonel got out of the jeep, he turned to Baker and said, "You're the only one with any continuity in the battalion," "I want you to come to battalion to be my S3 operations officer", Baker pointed out that he had only been in the unit 5 months. The new CO said, "your replacement will be here tomorrow morning!"

Baker was going to miss his unit. He had learned to enjoy being the commanding officer, He made arrangements to have Captain Blair transferred with him within a few weeks and packed his bags.

After the change of command ceremony the next day. Baker walked around and said goodbye to most of the people, His biggest surprise was a letter of appreciation from his two company clerks.

iv

At Phu Bai, Battalion headquarters, Baker shared the same hooch with the Battalion CO and the Executive Officer, The three would have access to the hot shower, a real flush toilet and a working air conditioner. Baker was halfway back to the real world again.

The T.O.C. (Tactical Operations Center) of the battalion was the nerve center for all the battery operations. Requests for ARA support came through Division Artillery, then to the battalion. ARA Missions were delegated from there to the three batteries.

After Captain Blair arrived, Major Baker also managed to get another West Pointer assigned to him in the T.O.C. Captain Charles Stanley had been an executive officer for B Battery and was available for staff assignment, When Baker requested Captain Stanley, LTC Novak smiled and said, "If you want to be a star, get stars to work for you!"

The Battalion Commander stopped Baker the next night in the club, "Baker, I noticed that you are a good printer, do you think you could put ARA in big red letters on the roof of the T.O.C?" Baker acknowledged that he could, and would do the job as soon as time permitted.

The T.O.C. was partially underground. It contained all of the radios for the fire net, maps of all of the operations plus intelligence data, Because of the security required, the center was completely surrounded with sandbags and a tin roof that was reinforced to stop mortars, There were no windows, and it was hot.

v

The battalion was between operations, It was a hot afternoon, Major Baker was sitting at his desk in the T.O.C. smoking a cigarette and listening to the battery radio traffic, Captain Blair was looking for a piece of paper in the files.

"Look at this Blair", Captain Blair watched as a fat fly slowly landed on Baker's desk. The fly sat still while Baker moved a heavy glass paper weight up behind him, slowly easing it over the fly, then capturing it under the indentation of the paperweight.

Baker and Blair studied the magnified fly for a few minutes, Baker took a small plastic straw and blew cigarette smoke under the glass paperweight, Both watched in fascination as the fly flipped over on it's back and crossed it's legs, "Damned, that just shows you how hazardous smoking can be!" Baker said.

The magnifying glass was removed, and as Baker and Blair were performing last rites, the fly suddenly twitched, shook it's head, scrarnbled back to it's feet and took off, Baker had a brainstorm!

Using the lightest manifold tissue paper that was available, Baker made narrow strips that came to a small point. On each one, Baker and Blair printed the names of the pilots, the operations people, and the radio telephone operator.

Once this was completed, airplane glue was located in one of the Red Cross packages.

Major Baker and Captain Blair devoted the rest of the afternoon to capturing every oversize Vietnamese fly that wandered into the T.O.C.

As each fly was captured, it would receive the nicotine anesthesia treatment. While under, the tissue paper was glued to the tail, Each fly soon became the proud owner of a banner which it towed around the T.O.C. Because the different sizes, each fly was a study in 'weight and balance'. Some flies, with longer banners, were constantly on the edge of a stall.

visitors frequently arrived for briefings. Often, a large fly would drift by, struggling to stay-airborne, and carrying the 2 inch long banner emblazoned with "Bob Baker" or maybe "Captain Blair".

If the visitor appeared to notice the fly, both Baker and Blair ignored it's existence, It was as if nothing unusual was taking place. Sometimes the visitor would leave after the briefing, shaking his head and wondering about his own sanity.

During one of the daily morning briefings conducted by the operations personnel, "Charles Stanley" slowly lumbered past the tip of the CD's nose, Charles was a small fly with a very large banner, and he was in danger of spinning in.

The Battalion Commander followed the fly with his gaze, stopping to look quizzically at Major Baker. Baker returned the CD's look with his best blank expression, as if to say, "is there something wrong?"

vi

That night, at the Officer's club, Baker was talking to Major Lynn, who was holding his sixth drink. Baker started slowly swaying from side to side. Finally, Lynn gave in, clutched his stomach and ran from the club.

The Battalion Commander approached Bob at the club, "Major Baker, I want you to dig out all the daily logs for the past six months to find out when the enemy rocket attacks occurred and what damage we had to our aircraft"

Crap! Baker thought to himself, there goes our study on weight and balance, He had clearly given Captain Blair instructions to formulate a plan for the use of two flies, and a bigger banner. Now, that would have to wait!

After returning to the hooch, the Battalion Commander explained to Baker that the new Division Artillery commander had a thing about aircraft availability, and there was some question about the enemy rocket attacks and the amount of damage they had caused.

Although the Division Artillery commander knew nothing about flying, he wanted 100 percent aircraft availability, Since he was not an aviator, he related helicopters to jeeps, That meant helicopters would have to stay away from ground fire and maintenance inspections would be performed on a running basis.

Baker poured over the reports from the past six months and entered the dates and damage on paper, As he studied the results, he began to notice a common modus operandi on the part of the enemy.

It was a known fact, When the Russian made 122 mm rockets hit the Division camp they came from the same group of hills west of Phu Bai. When this happened, all personnel would dive for bunkers, Baker would run for the T.O.C. and either A or B battery launched their hot section to pound the hillside with aerial rockets, And, in each case, the enemy would be long gone.

The long Russian made rockets were placed on the side of a small hill which provided the proper elevation to loft them into the Division area, The NVA soldiers carried the rockets in to the launch area, attached an electrical timing device to the rockets and would be miles away at launch time, By then, the ARA attack was an exercise in futility.

Baker completed the compilation of information, had it typed up and presented it to the Battalion Commander in the Officer's club that night. LTC Novak was reading the study when Baker suddenly announced, "the next rocket attack will be December 12th, plus or minus two days!"

LTC Novak looked up at Baker in disbelief, "what do you mean?" Baker explained that the rocket attacks had a definite pattern, The rockets were arriving in the Division area every 59 days, plus or minus two, Baker's supposition was; it took the NVA that long to haul them down the Ho Chi Minh trail and place them on the launch site.

The Battalion Commander did not want to believe Baker, Baker tendered a twenty dollar bet, the CO accepted. On the morning of December i4th, the Battalion Commander was paying the twenty dollars to Baker. Before the end of the next 59 day period, the ARA was airborne and in the vicinity of the the launch area prior to blastoff.

vii

R&R's (Rest and Recuperation) were available to all military personnel in South Viet Nam. Each month, certain recreational areas would be allocated to a unit. The Officer's and enlisted personnel drew their rest area out of a hat.

The areas included Tokyo, Hong Kong, Sidney Australia, Honolulu, Formosa and Bangkok. Baker had drawn Bangkok. He needed the rest, and it wouldn't hurt to get 'cuperated' while he was there.

Baker borrowed all of the money that Captain Blair had available, left strict instructions to come up with a feasibility study for a twin and possibly a tri fly powered banner towing service, then caught his flight for Bangkok.

Bangkok. City of 3 million people ruled by a constitutional monarchy and King Rama IX. Of more importance to Major Baker, Bangkok was the home of "The New Bangkok Massage Parlor". Baker had barely departed the steps from the aircraft before he was enroute to the famous massage parlor.

It was like standing in front of a candy store window. Baker stood there, eyes twitching, mouth salivating and groin hurting.

He was in front of a large plate glass window, looking into lighted room full of young girls, Each girl had a large number on a badge pinned to her uniform, Each girl was a typical 'Thai', short, dark and beautiful, Baker managed to stammer to the maitre d, "I'll have number seven on the menu please!"

The maitre d pushed the button for the intercom. "Number seven, rosy side up!" The four loot 7 inch girl left the lit room and entered the outer darkened room, Baker paid the 25 Bahts (5.00 U.S.) to the maitre d and followed number seven to her room.

The little Thai girl had picked up a wicker basket containing towels, soap and lotions. Once inside the room, Baker saw a. large bathtub, a small surgical table, and an operating table on wheels. Everything was white and spotless.

Baker followed his instructions to a 'T' as he removed his clothes. The Thai girl was filling the tub with hot water. As soon the tub was full, he was instructed to get in. Baker's joints began separating as the extreme hot water penetrated his body, The girl washed his hair, while crooning a Thai song.

The only thing that didn't loosen or soften up was immediately obvious when Baker stood to get the rest of his body washed. Once he was thoroughly clean, he was told to get on the table. Being a military man, Baker obeyed the order.

The girl massaged his shoulders, his spine, the small of his back and then started on his feet. Once around the ankles and the calves, the girl would slowly and only occasionally work her way up inside of his legs with a slight touch now and then, as if by error.

"Turn over!" The girl said. Baker was spring loaded, and almost knocked the little girl over as he flipped to his sunny side up.

Slowly, the girl worked on Baker's ankles, his inner calves and thighs and then moved to his shoulders and pectorals, then back again to his inner thighs with that occasional hint of more, Baker had reached a state of explosiveness that was nearly uncontrollable.

Without Baker realizing it, the girl quickly reached behind to the surgical table and dipped her hand into a large jar of vaseline. When she grabbed Baker, he yelled "Oooohh Noooo!!!" She replied, "Oh Yes, it is good for your body!" In two quick swipes, it was over with, Baker would never again argue with medical facts.

Bangkok was loaded with bars, nightclubs and bargains galore. Anything could be seen or had in Bangkok for the right price, And the prices were usually right.

The exchange rate of 5 to 1 made it possible for a GI to have a girl stay him for 5 days for as little as 25.00 dollars. She stayed with him night and day, she ate with him, slept with him and even argued over the merchants prices for him, In most cases she more than made up for the 25.00 investment.

Massage parlors were everywhere. The oriental is a strong believer in massages and the women of Bangkok were taught from a very young age how to please a man with what "is good for the body".

The five days in Bangkok were over and it was time to return to South Viet Nam and the Battalion. Baker had shopped, and stopped in at the New Bangkok Massage Parlor several more times for a brief visit with number seven.

The night of his return to Phu Bai, Baker told Major Lynn of his experience in Bangkok, While he talked, Baker swayed gently from side to side building tempo until Lynn doubled over and gagged on his way out of the Officer's club, Pavlov's pup, Baker thought, I'll have to remember to send Lynn a picture of a ship when I get home.

viii

It was a casual statement by Major Baker to Captain Blair, "It's too bad you can't see the Army Navy game this year!" "But I can", replied Blair, "they're playing it in Da Nang this year", Baker went on, "we should do something about getting reserved seats for the battalion!".

The stadium plan was drawn showing the reserved section for the 4/77th ARA, The section was on the 50 yard line. A note above the plan stated that each interested party had to sign up to qualify for the seating, The plan, and sign in sheet, was tacked to a. support post in the T.O.C.

A visiting Colonel arrived for a briefing in the operations center, After the briefing explaining the merits of ARA and its capabilities, the Colonel was shown around the T.O.C. He stopped, looked at the sign in sheet for the football game and placed his name on the list, Baker and Blair would always wonder if he showed up in Da Nang looking for the stadium.

"Baker, where is my big ARA sign for the roof of the T.O.C.?" Baker told the Battalion CO that he would do it as soon as time permitted, and as soon as he could locate the right brush.

ix

Major Baker and Captain Blair rounded up the ten pilots for Camp Evans, The UH1H was loaded, and so were the passengers. Baker and Blair were to return the pilots to the Griffin pad after the hail and farewell party, The party had been a big success for Major Baker., he had won forty dollars at the crap table and managed to get Major Lynn sick one more time.

It was a dark moonless night as the UH1H took off from the Battalion enroute to Camp Evans. The aircraft just turned north when the artillery started firing a. night illumination mission outside the Evans perimeter. Baker and Blair watched as the rounds ignited in the high arc where the parachute deployed, each bright white round lazily drifting to earth.

The illumination rounds were mesmerizing. The mission continued, lighting up the countryside just outside of Camp Evans where someone had detected movement.

All at once, the illumination rounds stopped. Baker and Blair had not anticipated and end of mission. Their pupils had snapped tightly shut, as they watched the bright illumination flares.

The UH1H continued north. Captain Blair was flying from the left seat. Major Baker looked at the instruments on the panel and noticed the altimeter beginning to show a loss of altitude. The turn and bank indicator was indicating a turn to the right and the VSI (verticle speed indicator) was showing the aircraft in a. 500 foot per minute descent. Baker put his foot on the floor button for the intercom and said, "how are you doing Blair, everything o.k.?"

Captain Blair replied, "everything is fine!". Baker took the controls and said, "I've got the aircraft!". Captain Blair looked puzzled as he released his grip on the controls. Major Baker continued the right turn and descent. He leveled off and stopped the turn on a heading back to the battalion.

Blair had experienced a severe case of vertigo without realizing it. The severe darkness of South Viet Nam was hard to contend with under normal conditions. With the pupils the size of pin heads, it was impossible. Baker had watched the instruments start to indicate that they were in a lazy spiral to the ground.

On the ground, the pilots were told that they would spend the night in Battalion. Captain Blair was not aware of how severe his vertigo had been. Blair had refused to believe the instruments, his senses told him that he was straight and level.

X

Because of the high interest in aircraft availability, and the Division Artillery Commanders lack of understanding regarding maintenance requirements for helicopters, a daily briefing was conducted by Captain Harris.

The maintenance briefing followed the operational briefing each morning. Captain Harris would go through each aircraft status, what was being done to keep it flyable and what couldn't be done to prevent a down condition. The Battalion Commander was under pressure from above and had to answer for each downed aircraft.

Captain Harris was a big, easy going likeable man. Fortunately. Major Baker, Captain Blair and Captain Stanley made it a point to screw up some part of his briefing, on a daily basis.

Small changes on the Captain's briefing board was one method. The board contained a 'remarks' section, If the aircraft was down for engine change, or other reasons, it would be entered in the remarks.

The maintenance captain had a sergeant who posted the board on a daily basis. The addition of a phrase in the remarks section would drive him wild. For instance, 'lexinator change', or 'spotter bar inop.' would cause a great deal of discussion, since these were nonexistent parts.

Captain Blair received a pair of plastic horns with attached suction cups from his wife. It was several months after Halloween, but that didn't matter. Blair had a use for them.

The maintenance Captain was just beginning his daily briefing regarding the aircraft status. He was using the pointer to indicate each aircraft and the problems.

With his best 'Alfred E. Newman' smile and the horns in place on his forehead, Captain Blair raised up from behind the seats at the rear of the briefing room.

Captain Harris completely lost control at this point as he looked up to see, 'what, me care?' with the bright yellow horns protruding from his forehead. The aircraft briefing was lost as the Captain fell to the floor holding his stomach and gasping for breath.

xi

Captain Blair stood silently by as Major Baker said, "I don't care what you say, it's bound to work!" "The four flies abreast on this light Piece of balsa will be as good as any B52" "Now if I can get them to fly over to A battery and shit on Major Lynn, I'll be happy!"

Baker released the new flying concept. The flies on the left wing decided to rest and the right two flies were at maximum RPM's. The entire machine spun in on the spot. Captain Blair assumed his 'I told you so look'.

xii

The hail and farewell for Major Baker was three weeks before his departure. It had been a decent tour. During the entire year, Baker had not taken one hit in an aircraft, and he had managed to perfect his knowledge of aerodynamics.

During the party afterwards, LTC Novak approached Major Baker and asked, "are you going to start my ARA sign on the T.O.C. now?" Baker said yes, since the new S3 was in the job, he would have plenty of time.

In a few days, LTC Novak asked, "why did it take you so long to start my sign?" Baker told him. The letters for the ARA would be twenty feet high and would be seen by everyone for miles around, to include the NVA rocketeers on the hills. Baker didn't want to be near the T.O.C. by the time the next shipment of Russian rockets arrived from Hanoi.

Baker was on the big silver jet, heading back to the real world. As he tried to capture the fly that was near him, he thought of the big red 'ARA' drying on the roof of the T.O.C.

BACKWARD

Although some liberties have been taken, most of what you have just read is true. Names and dates are fictitious to preclude injured feelings or embarrassment.

There may be some criticism from those who were there. Not all was quite as light as the author portrayed it in some passages. But in some cases, it had to have been even lighter.

There were many units that had it much worse than others. And yet, there were individuals and units in support missions that barely knew they were in a war zone, This is going to be true in any conflict.

Many of the career military personnel involved in the Viet Nam conflict feel that too much pressure was brought to bear from the home front. A very small group of dissenters caught the attention of the media. Because of the anti Viet Nam feeling that ensued, the resulting restrictions placed upon the troops, the conflict became a lost cause.

Those of you that fit in the category of following the lead of those few, the ones that had the money and backing to get media attention, are nothing more than sheep.

The author was honored to have had the chance to fight when asked to do so. To balk, or complain would have gone completely against his convictions as an American.

Made in the USA
Lexington, KY
30 July 2013